"Come on," Damon argued. "Your being around didn't have anything to do with that kid going crazy."

Jenna knew he was right. They chatted for a while longer, about what they'd gotten for Christmas and when Damon would be back on campus. Classes resumed in two weeks, but dorms reopened several days earlier. Jenna planned to go back the first day she'd be able.

"I promised my mom we'd have dinner with her as soon as you're back," she told him.

"I look forward to it," Damon replied. "She seems nice."

"Of course. She's my mom."

The doorbell rang then, and she promised to call Damon the following day; then she hung up quickly. When she went into the living room, she saw her mother holding the door open in an obvious state of distress. Moira stood in the open door, her arms wrapped around her belly.

"Moi?" Jenna ventured. "What happened?"

Somehow, she knew what the answer was going to be.

"It happened again," Moira said, wiping away tears. "John Gage killed his family last night."

christopher golden
HEAD GAMES

A *Body of Evidence*
thriller starring Jenna Blake

POCKET PULSE
New York   London   Toronto   Sydney   Singapore

An *Original* Publication of POCKET BOOKS

 POCKET PULSE published by
Pocket Books, a division of Simon & Schuster Inc.
1230 Avenue of the Americas, New York, NY 10020

ISBN: 0-671-77582-0

First Pocket Pulse printing June 2000

10 9 8 7 6 5 4 3 2 1

POCKET PULSE and colophon are trademarks of
Simon & Schuster Inc.

Front cover illustration by Kamil Vojnar

Printed in the U.S.A.

for Kiera O'Neil and Gerilyn Deveaux

acknowledgments

Thanks, as always, to my agent, Lori Perkins; to my editor, Lisa Clancy, and her assistant, Micol Ostow; and to my family: Connie, Nicholas, and Daniel. Special thanks to Dr. Dean Pappas for his invaluable input.

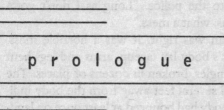

prologue

Not long after dawn, two days before Christmas, Jenna Blake stood over the shattered, nearly unrecognizable corpse of the mayor of Somerset, Massachusetts, and took deep breaths to keep from throwing up. The day was gray and cold, threatening snow—Jenna could almost taste it in the air—and the lights from the police cars seemed dull and muted. Powerless. Yellow police tape stretched from a large blue Dumpster to the stone column on one side of the rear stairs of City Hall. Both entrances to the parking lot were blocked by police vehicles to keep civilians from the crime scene.

But, surreal as it seemed to her, Jenna was there. She had never met Jim Kerchak, the mayor, before his death. Now she found herself wondering if he'd been any good at his job, or if maybe he hadn't been, and that truth led him to take his own life.

A custodian had found Mayor Kerchak's remains just after four o'clock in the morning.

"I'll tell ya what ya wanna know," the man said in his statement to the police. "Long as I don't gotta clean it up. Jesus, what a mess."

The custodian was right. It was a horrible mess. Mayor Kerchak's body lay faceup, arms and legs bent at impossible angles, broken in dozens of places. The splash of blood several feet away from the body indicated that the body had bounced at least once on landing. The back of the mayor's skull had been turned into bone shrapnel, the rest of him just a ravaged pulp of blood and skin, in what had once been a very nice suit.

Jim Kerchak had been a snappy dresser.

During the night the custodian had discovered the door to the roof of City Hall standing open. One glance over the edge of the roof told him the story, but he had no idea it was the mayor until minutes after his frantic 911 call, when he made his way downstairs and outside. It seemed obvious that Kerchak had done himself in with a swan dive off the roof, but Jenna had been taught, almost from day one on the job, never to make any judgments about a corpse until an autopsy had been performed.

As she managed to get her gag reflex under control and choke down the burning bile that rose in the back of her throat at the sight of the mayor's brains smeared on the pavement, Jenna turned to look at the man who had taught her that lesson: Dr. Walter Slikowski.

Slick, as she thought of him (but would never call him to his face), was the county medical examiner and widely respected in the field. Local law enforcement often asked him for assistance above and beyond the call of duty. At that moment, she saw, he was deep in thought, brow furrowed in contemplation. Whatever he was thinking, she could tell by his expression that it wasn't pleasant.

How could it be? His friend is dead.

It had come as a surprise to her that Slick and Kerchak had been friends, but it shouldn't have. Both men had very little life outside their jobs. The general feeling seemed to be that Kerchak had been a good mayor. Given her opinion of Slick, Jenna was inclined to believe that.

"What do you think?" she asked quietly.

For a moment Slick only sat in his wheelchair and stared at the corpse. She thought he was studying what remained of Mayor Kerchak's face. The man's neck was broken, head bent at an odd angle. The back of his skull had been destroyed, but the way he had struck the ground, the edge of his cheek, from temple to jaw, had also been pulverized. That part of his face was nothing but pulp—bone and muscle and skin turned to jelly. Jenna thought the white bit she saw jutting from the mess was an edge of shattered jawbone, but she dared not look close enough to confirm that. Her control over the urge to vomit was tenuous at best.

Dr. Slikowski let out a slow breath and shook his head. He was fortyish and thin, with graying hair and wire-rim glasses that gave him an air of hipness that was dispelled as soon as one had a conversation with him. He was a brilliant man, and his mind was always working, which could make him seem distant or distracted when speaking. There was a kind of propriety about him that was almost European, though he had been born and raised in New England.

He still hadn't responded to Jenna's question. She was about to ask again, to tap his shoulder and try to drag his attention away from the horrid remains of his friend, when Audrey Gaines slipped under the yellow police tape and strode over to them. Jenna glanced around for Audrey's partner, Danny Mariano, but didn't see him. The two were homicide detectives in Somerset, and Jenna and Dr. Slikowski had had ample opportunity to get to know them.

"Hello, Walter," Audrey said, with what passed for compassion from her but would have seemed coldness from anyone else.

"Audrey."

"We can talk later. I just wanted to tell you I'm sorry. I know you and the mayor were friendly."

Slick smiled. "Once upon a time," he said. "Frankly, neither of us had much chance to socialize of late. But thank you. Have you established what you'll tell the press?"

Audrey took a breath, hesitating. Jenna was surprised. Audrey Gaines rarely hesitated about anything.

"For the moment we're only confirming that he's dead and that the investigation is ongoing. After the autopsy, we can give them some more."

"All right," Slick said and nodded. "I'll do it this afternoon."

"Are you sure that's a good idea, Walter?" Audrey asked. "Maybe somebody else ought to take this one."

Slick turned to look at the detective, frowning. "Are you trying to tell me my job, Detective Gaines?"

Audrey blinked once, then offered a tiny, almost imperceptible shrug. "I'll call you later today, then," she said. She turned away from them and went to speak to one of the forensic specialists, a portly man who was in the midst of analyzing the impact point several feet away.

Jenna wanted to say something, to offer some words of comfort, but nothing would come. Audrey was probably right. Psychologically, it was a bad idea for Slick to do an autopsy on a man he'd called friend. Once upon a time, in a horrid nightmare that she frequently wished was only that, and not an actual memory, Jenna had walked in on the autopsy of her own best friend, unaware that Melody was even dead. She had never gotten over that moment, and doubted that she ever would.

On the other hand, she knew Slick. A part of him simply couldn't allow anyone else to autopsy Jim Kerchak—mainly because the M.E. didn't trust anyone else to do the job right.

Jenna wanted to say something.

More than that, she wanted to go home. Home to her mother's house, rather than back to campus. *I wonder how long before I stop thinking of Mom's as home,* she thought.

The next day would be Christmas Eve. Almost everyone else on campus was gone already, including her boyfriend, Damon Harris, and her two best friends, Yoshiko—who was Jenna's roommate—and her boyfriend, Hunter. Finals were over and the dorm was abandoned, the campus almost a ghost town.

Jenna had intended to go into work that morning, transcribe the audio records of the two autopsies from the previous day, and go back to her mother's in Natick. It was all set. Her father, Frank Logan, and his fiancée, Shayna Emerson—both of whom were professors at Somerset—had left the previous day for a sabbatical in France. Frank lent Jenna his car while they were gone. Freshmen weren't supposed to have cars on campus, but it wasn't really *her* car and, with his faculty sticker, she could park almost anywhere.

She'd had it all worked out.

Then the phone had rung, long before the gray dawn, and Jenna was awakened with a start. That early, she knew, a phone call could not be good news. Slick was on the line, with the news of the mayor's death. Now this. Jenna thought she should try to convince him that Kerchak's autopsy should be handled by someone else, for his sake, but also for her own.

She didn't need this, not when the campus felt like the Twilight Zone. Her things were already packed, except for the antique perfume bottle she had bought in Harvard Square in Cambridge as a Christmas present for her mother. It was in a box, but she didn't have any wrapping paper, and if she waited much longer to go to the drugstore to buy some, Jenna was afraid she'd end up with Daffy Duck birthday paper or something.

Someone shouted behind her, and Jenna glanced around quickly. A cameraman from Channel 7 was trying to push past the cops blocking his path. The blue lights from the police cars painted pale ghosts on the stone wall of City Hall.

"Jenna, what is it?" Slick asked.

She looked at him again, surprised to find him watching her. He'd seemed so lost in his own thoughts, in his sorrow. Jenna opened her mouth to tell him she had to go, that an autopsy wasn't on her personal holiday agenda. Those weren't the words that came out of her mouth, though.

"I'll assist you," she told Slick, much to her own astonishment.

The M.E. shook his head. "You should get home to your mother. I'm sure you have plans for Christmas."

Yes. Go home. He told you to go, and you have to wrap Mom's present. Those were her thoughts. But her words . . . her words were different.

"I can go later," she said, mentally cursing herself. "Dyson and Doug are on their way to Aruba by now. I know you don't technically need the help, and I'm no doctor anyway, but I know that things go faster when you have someone with you."

Slick couldn't argue with that. "All right. Let's hurry, though. The last thing I want is for April Blake to blame me for interfering with her holiday plans."

"She can blame the mayor," Jenna replied.

Slick looked grimly down at the man's corpse. He nodded, spun his chair around and began to propel it back toward his van. Jenna followed, ignoring the cops and the press and the nagging voice in the back of her mind that kept saying *wrapping paper* over and over.

*　　*　　*

"Tell me what you see."

Jenna was in the middle of using a scalpel to harvest a small sample of Mayor Kerchak's heart tissue. She glanced over at Slick and saw that he was not looking at her, or at the heart she was cutting, but at the cadaver on the stainless steel table in the center of the autopsy room. Under the lights, the dead man was even more horrible to look at than he had been before: where the skin was unbruised it was pale and pasty, like some hideous wax museum dummy.

"What do you mean?" Jenna asked.

Slick nodded at the dead man. "Something's odd here. I was just wondering if you had noticed it."

Jenna managed the tiniest grin. It was a test. When she had taken the job as pathology assistant at Somerset Medical Center, she was supposed to do mostly clerical work. Over time, however, as Slick had realized that her interest in solving puzzles and her intuition were similar in some ways to his own, theirs had grown into a kind of mentor/student relationship. Jenna's job description hadn't been merely clerical for months.

With another glance at Slick, hoping for some clue from the angle of his gaze, Jenna stepped away from the scale and the partially dissected heart, and began to move around the steel table. It was canted slightly, to allow easier access for Slick in his wheelchair.

As she worked her way to the other side of the table, she examined the chest cavity, opened wide by a Y-incision. Nothing out of place there, as far as she could see. Dr. Slikowski had yet to get to the brain, so there was nothing for her to notice there. The entire front of the body was bruised a deep purple, from toes to genitals to chest. Even part of one cheek, the one not damaged by the impact with the pavement, was flushed almost black. Jenna thought Jim Kerchak might have bounced more than once, given the bruises on him. They . . .

Those aren't bruises.

The realization came suddenly, and her eyes flew open wide as she moved closer to study the body. Jenna paid special attention to the shattered parts of the skull, including the right temple and jaw.

"There wasn't much blood at the site, was there?" she asked.

"Not very much, no," Slick replied grimly.

Jenna nodded. "I'm with you now."

"Elaborate, if you don't mind," Slick prodded, still testing her.

"I thought it was all bruises from the impact, but the dark 'bruising' is the effect of the settling of the blood after death," she said. "Can't remember what it's called."

"Dependent lividity." Slick smiled softly and nodded for her to continue.

"The body was faceup when it was discovered," Jenna said. "His back and bones and the side of his head were badly damaged by the impact, but that wouldn't account for this. The only way dependent lividity would have happened in this way, with all the blood settling to the front of his body, is if he was killed much earlier, the body left facedown for hours, and *then* thrown off the roof, where he would eventually be found faceup."

"I think we'll find that his neck was broken," Slick explained. "Of course, only finishing the autopsy will allow us to confirm that." The medical examiner smiled. "Well done, Jenna. I'm proud of you. Now let me finish up down here. You get on home."

Uncomfortably, Jenna shifted her weight. "Are you sure?"

"Very. I'll take it from here. Go home and enjoy your Christmas. You've earned it."

"Okay," she agreed, stripping off her bloody gloves and slipping out of her white lab coat. "But while Dyson's away, if you really need my help, just call and I'll come right out, okay? I have my dad's car, so it's no problem."

"I'll do that. You go on. Drive safely and Merry Christmas."

Jenna dropped her lab coat on a pile of laundry. As she pushed out the door, she called back to him, "Merry Christmas to you, too, Dr. Slikowski."

Slick barely acknowledged her, his attention back on the corpse of his friend, the mayor, who it now seemed had been murdered. Any trace of a smile had been erased from Slick's face.

In that moment it seemed impossible to Jenna that Christmas was only two days away.

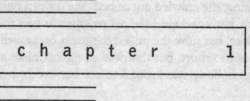

chapter 1

When Jenna's eyes slowly opened on the morning of December 24, it took her a moment to realize where she was. This was not her dorm room in Sparrow Hall. Home, then. Her old bed, in her old room, in her mother's house.

There was a New Orleans carnival mask on the wall above her head, pink and purple, with a blue ribbon hanging down the back. Asian fans were splayed on either side of the mirror above the heavy wooden bureau across from her bed. Scattered around the mirror were concert ticket stubs, pages from *Teen People*, and photos of her best friends from high school.

It was so very real, so vivid, but for a few precious seconds, as she lay blinking her eyes, Jenna wasn't sure if she was awake or dreaming. From somewhere, she smelled coffee, and a broad smile stretched across her face.

Home, she thought again. And then her eyes went

11

wide and she grinned even more broadly. *Christmas Eve.*

Stretching, she crawled out of bed. She'd worn only the top of her checkered flannel pajamas to bed the night before, but now she pulled the pants on as well. They were too short, but that was all right. Unlike at the dorm, nobody was around to see her except her mother.

Jenna checked her watch, which lay on the bureau. It was almost nine-thirty. Curious, she went out into the hall and down the stairs. In the kitchen, she found her mother reading the paper in a terry robe and ragged slippers. April Blake sipped at her coffee as she paged through the Living section of the *Boston Globe.*

"Hey," Jenna rasped, then cleared her throat.

April almost spilled her coffee. Then she laughed. "Honey, you startled me."

Jenna kissed her mother's head, then slid into a chair across from her. "I guess I did. Maybe you're getting too comfortable having the house all to yourself." She grinned. "And speaking of comfortable, those are definitely not work clothes. You staying home today?"

"Actually, I have one surgery this afternoon—a malignant tumor on Don Morris's right lung. But when I get back, it's eggnog and *Miracle on 34th Street,* right? Unless you want to do that tomorrow night."

For a moment Jenna studied her mother, wondering if the suggestion was genuine, or just courtesy. She couldn't tell.

"You know, tomorrow might not be a bad idea," she ventured. "I mean, I haven't seen Moira in forever, and Priya was weird at Thanksgiving. It'd be cool just to hang out."

"If their parents will let them," April replied, arching an eyebrow. "Not everyone has a mom as flexible as yours. But, okay, tomorrow night is eggnog and *Miracle*. We're going to your uncle Brian's after you open all the presents Santa brought you."

Jenna rolled her eyes. "Never too old for Santa, huh?"

"Never," April said firmly.

"Well, he got you a little something, too," Jenna told her mother. "But that was before he knew we were going to Uncle Brian's. Now you might end up with coal in your stocking."

April's expression was half grin, half frown. "You love Brian."

Jenna shrugged. "I do. I just . . . it's Christmas, y'know? I'd rather be in my own house. Too bad they couldn't come here."

"Next year," April promised. "It was just too much for me, trying to get ready for that many people. I used to have a servant girl around here to help out, but I sold her to the local college."

"And on *that* note . . ." Jenna sighed and rose from her chair, then walked to the fridge to fetch a glass of orange juice.

"By the way, while you were sleeping in, you had a phone call," her mother said. "Noah. He's home. Wants you to call him back."

Jenna nodded. *Of course he does*, she thought. *That's just what I need, the one guy capable of making any reunion with my old friends supremely uncomfortable.*

"I'll call him after I take a shower."

Jenna wasn't looking forward to it. Not that she didn't like Noah. She even loved him, in a way. They had been friends for eight years, ever since Noah had moved to Natick, Massachusetts, from Buffalo, New York. But in high school, he had made her life miserable. That was a pretty selfish way of looking at things, she knew, but high school wasn't exactly a rational time in a young person's life. Moira, Priya, and Jenna had been the three musketeers. All for one, and one for all.

The problem was, that was never meant to extend to guys. Moira had gone out with Noah all through her sophomore and junior years, but then they had a huge blowup and broke up. At the beginning of senior year, Noah asked Priya out, and she committed the cardinal sin of saying yes. Things were never the same with any of them after that.

During senior year, Jenna was torn between her two closest friends. Only near the end of that year, when Priya dumped Noah, did the girls finally begin to mend their friendship. By then, of course, high school was almost over.

They cried and hugged and promised one another that they'd always be friends, that they'd never grow apart. But then Moira had gone to film school at the University of Southern California, and Priya had taken off for Northwestern, in Illinois, and the future had begun. Life had moved on. Jenna had kept in touch by e-mail with her friends—including Noah, who was at UMass, Amherst—but things changed so quickly.

Though only seven months had passed since graduation, what had been important in high school seemed like only a memory now. Jenna's life had been drastically altered. She had new friends, a new relationship with her father, new hopes and dreams that her old friends didn't share and might not even understand. They certainly didn't understand why she was working as a pathology assistant.

Jenna loved them all, no question about that. And she had missed them. The idea of seeing them—and some of her other high school friends—filled her with excitement. But among her emotions there was also a certain amount of trepidation. Jenna had to wonder if, now that they were in college, they would have anything other than the past in common.

"Are you all right, Jenna?" her mother asked, a frown deepening the lines of her face. "Something particularly gruesome at work? Or just fretting about how you did on your finals?"

"None of the above," Jenna promised. "It's just going to be weird seeing everybody again."

"It's only been a few months," her mother noted, bemused now.

"I guess," Jenna replied. She didn't want to have to try to explain all her feelings to her mother. "As for gruesome, we did have a wicked nasty one yesterday. Jim Kerchak?"

April looked surprised. "Somerset's mayor? I saw that on the news."

"That's me, ambulance chaser." Jenna laughed. "Slick says 'hello,' by the way."

"Great," her mother grumbled. "When you talk to

him, tell him if he doesn't watch out for my daughter, I'll have to kill him."

"Please don't," Jenna begged. "I'd probably end up doing the autopsy."

"That isn't funny, it's ghoulish."

Jenna looked at her mother evenly. "It wasn't meant to be funny."

There was a brief halt to the conversation. When it started up again, they moved on to more pleasant topics of conversation. Her mother had had a couple of dates with a new doctor at the hospital named Ken Crowther. Ken was a heart surgeon, which led Jenna to make a few painfully bad romantic-doctor jokes. According to April, the dates with Ken had been nice. They'd even been to the movies, which astonished Jenna. She didn't think her mother had seen a movie that wasn't on tape in a couple of years.

"Great. Now you'll take off for Europe to plan *your* wedding, too."

April scoffed. "Don't rush me, daughter. I haven't done more than kiss him yet."

"Yow!" Jenna cried, and held up a hand. "Halt! Stop right there. That information is on a need-to-know basis, and trust me . . . I *don't* need to know."

"What about you and Damon?" April went on.

"Have we done more than kiss?" Jenna replied, horrified by the question. "Again, need to know?"

A wistful, almost sad expression came over April's features. "You used to tell me everything."

"Back then, I didn't have anything to tell," Jenna teased.

"What's that supposed to mean?" April studied her closely.

"It means I desperately need Eggo waffles for breakfast."

After the waffles, Jenna went back upstairs and showered. In her room, she searched through her closet, looking for something to wear that she hadn't brought to Somerset with her. Something different to wear. She found an olive turtleneck and a pair of khakis that weren't badly wrinkled. When she pulled them down off the shelf, her old navy-blue Natick High sweatshirt fell down on her head.

For a moment, Jenna hugged the old sweatshirt and thought about her friends and how much she really had missed them. When she glanced up at her image in the mirror and brushed a strand of her still-damp auburn hair away from her face, she noticed that her eyes brimmed with tears in spite of her contented smile.

Jenna didn't cry, not really. But she came close, and she wasn't sure exactly why. All she did know was that when she went back to Somerset two weeks later, she planned to have that sweatshirt with her.

Before she even finished dressing, Jenna heard the phone ring downstairs. A moment later her mother's footsteps sounded on the stairs. "That's Moira," April called from the top step.

Jenna went into her mother's room to answer the phone. She lay across the bed, her feet dangling over the edge. In that position, she felt the rightness of being at home even more than she had while sleeping in her own bed.

"Hey!" she said excitedly as she answered.

"Jesus, Blake, were you *ever* gonna call me?" Moira chided her.

"I just got outta the shower, Moi. Gimme a break, all right?"

"When'd you get home?"

"Late last night," Jenna replied.

She considered telling Moira she had come home late because of Mayor Kerchak's autopsy, but then thought better of it. She knew it would freak Moira out, and this vacation was about reconnecting with her old friends, not alienating them.

"How'd you do on your finals?"

"Pretty good, I guess. I hope," Jenna said tentatively. "I was dreading the bio exam, but I think I did really well. Actually looking forward to taking Gross Anatomy next semester."

"Better you than me," Moira said. "Maybe the doctor thing is in the blood."

"How'd you do?"

"I'm the female Spielberg. Nobody told you?" Moira joked. "Hey, did Noah call you yet?"

Jenna frowned. "This morning, but I was sleeping in. I'm a woman of leisure. Why, what's going on?"

"I'm having a party tonight. My parents said I could use the barn. Not a ton of people. The usual suspects, y'know? Well, all except for Priya," Moira explained. The latter bit she said with a kind of melancholy in her voice.

"What?" Jenna asked. "What's up with Priya?"

"I don't know," Moira sighed. "I've only talked to

18

her once since I got home. She's being really weird. I'd say bitchy, but it isn't that. She doesn't sound good, J. Noah left her two messages, but she hasn't called him back either."

Before Moira could ask her to do it, Jenna volunteered to call. "Maybe she'll listen to me. I wasn't part of your little soap opera, remember?"

"Bite me, Blake."

"Sorry, Kearney, you're not my type."

Both girls were laughing as they hung up. Jenna dialed Noah's immediately, but she got the answering machine. She figured he was out with his parents, maybe at the movies. The Levines were Jewish. As long as Jenna had known them, the entire family had always spent Christmas one of two ways. Either they went off to the Virgin Islands for a week, or they spent two or three days going to movies to avoid all the Christmas shows on television. On December 25, they ate Chinese food.

Noah had been to plenty of Christmas parties and seen plenty of inane Christmas specials, and so had his two younger brothers, but none of them was about to do anything that remotely seemed as if he were actually celebrating Christmas. The boys' parents would be furious. Of course, since neither of Noah's two significant girlfriends in high school had been Jewish, he had a pretty open mind about religion.

Especially when there was a party involved.

Jenna left Noah a message telling him what she planned to do. Then she grabbed her keys from the top of her bureau and went back down the stairs. Her mother was baking something that smelled especially good to take to Uncle Brian's the next day.

"Aren't you going to be late?" Jenna asked.

April gave her a doubtful smile. "I'll manage, somehow, to get to the hospital on time. I'll make it. You off to Moira's already?"

"Priya's, actually," Jenna told her. "Moira's having some people over tonight, and Priya's being all weird. Anyway . . . So, are we having dinner tonight?"

"If you can cram it into your busy schedule," her mother teased. "Now that you have your father's car, I get the feeling you're going to be around about as much as he used to be."

"Hey!" Jenna protested.

"Joking," April said, holding up her hands in surrender. "I was thinking about making that Louisiana chicken and dumplings tonight. Interested?"

Jenna smiled. "You spoil me."

"Yep."

The Lahiris' house was on Russell Road, a nicely wooded neighborhood that had once been among the wealthiest in Natick. Since then, new luxury developments had gone up in several places, but Russell Road was still a desirable area. The Lahiris lived in an antique-looking colonial set into a hill that sloped away from the road.

It was a quarter past eleven when Jenna pulled into the long driveway in front of the big house. There were no cars there, which was no significant surprise. Given that they weren't Christian, it was quite likely

Priya's parents would be working a full day on Christmas Eve.

On the porch, she rang the doorbell twice and waited. It felt strange, standing there so exposed. Though the house seemed empty, she was almost certain Priya was inside. Whatever was going on with her friend, Jenna wanted to help. But she didn't want to push herself on Priya, either. She waited a minute and then opened the storm door and knocked heavily. Another thirty seconds went by before she knocked again, but this time she didn't wait. When there was no immediate response, Jenna turned to start back down the path.

Behind her, the door swung open with a creak of hinges.

Jenna turned, both surprised and pleased, but the latter emotion only lasted until she got a look at the figure in the doorway. In the photographs around Jenna's bedroom mirror, and in her mind, Priya was one of the happiest, liveliest girls she had ever met. Though petite—she stood barely five feet tall and weighed no more than one hundred pounds—her energy and charisma, her personality, had always made her seem larger than life. It didn't hurt that, with her deep brown eyes, lush hair, and dark skin, she had an exotic beauty that never failed to attract attention.

The girl who stood in the doorway, dressed in a thin cotton nightshirt, was nothing like the Priya in the pictures or in Jenna's memory. She was still tiny, but now she looked unhealthy. Jenna thought about the whole

21

Kate Moss starving-chic look. Priya seemed pale, her hair was a mess, and her eyes were rimmed with red as if she'd been crying.

"Pri?"

"Hey," Priya said weakly.

Jenna went to the door and pulled Priya into her arms. As she did, she thought she caught, in her peripheral vision, the shadow of a smile on Priya's features.

"You look like shit, Lahiri," she whispered, her voice cracking with emotion. "What's going on with you?"

Priya actually laughed. "Wow. Cut to the chase, why don't you, J?" She pulled away from Jenna, the sadness on her face painful to look at. "Come inside. I don't want to give Jimmy Cunningham across the street a thrill."

There was an opening for a joke there, but Jenna couldn't summon up the energy for it. When Priya turned and walked inside, she followed. In the kitchen, Priya faced her again.

"I'm gonna have some O.J. You want anything?"

Jenna shrugged. "Something caffeinated, I guess."

As Priya went to the fridge and pulled out the orange juice and a two-liter bottle of Pepsi, Jenna went to the cabinet just to the left of the sink and took down two glasses. She knew the Lahiris' house almost as well as she did her own. In some ways, it was an extension of home.

When they were seated with their drinks at the kitchen table, Jenna waited for Priya to say something.

The other girl couldn't seem to meet her gaze. Finally Jenna said the words that had been in her head since Priya had answered the door.

"Pri, are you anorexic?"

With a startled look, Priya sat up straight. Then she laughed. "No, Jenna. I'm not anorexic."

Relief flooded over Jenna. But she went on.

"Bulimic?"

Priya didn't laugh this time. Instead, she looked pained. When she met Jenna's gaze again, there was a kind of embarrassment on her face that Jenna had never seen before.

"I've been home since Thanksgiving," Priya said.

Jenna didn't understand. She stared at Priya, trying to figure that one out. She'd exchanged e-mail with her friend in the month since then, and not once had Priya let on that she wasn't at Northwestern.

She isn't at Northwestern, Jenna thought, the words repeating themselves a couple of times in her mind. She remembered that Priya's e-mail address was a personal one, not a school account. And she began to understand.

"What happened?" she asked.

Priya glanced away, unwilling to look at her. When she spoke, her voice was barely a whisper.

"I guess I kinda quit."

When the screen door to the Gage family's back porch was ripped open, it made almost no sound at all. The door between the porch and the main house was locked. There was no alarm in the house, however, so that when the window over the kitchen sink—the one that looked out on the porch—was opened, no one was the wiser.

Inside the house, on that cold blue day before Christmas, the visitor moved in silence. Before the visitor left, the window in the kitchen would be closed. No one would notice the tear in the porch screen door. At least, not right away.

Visitor was the appropriate word. *Burglar* would have been inaccurate, for nothing was stolen from the Gages' home. Nor had anything been taken from any of the many other homes the visitor had surreptitiously entered in the past several days. It was extraordinary how, in an era of paranoia and fear, and the crime that caused it, so many people still left their homes unprotected. Unlocked, or even open, windows. No alarms. Incredibly enough, several of the homes the visitor had entered had actually had garage or back doors that had been left unlocked.

In the chaos of Christmas, no one would notice that the visitor had been there. As long as nothing was broken, or stolen . . . and the visitor was always very careful about that. No, nothing stolen. Quite the opposite, in fact.

The visitor took nothing. Instead, when the house was empty again, the intrusion complete, something had been added to the contents of the house. Something wrapped in brightly colored paper and red-and-white ribbon. A gift under the Christmas tree, with all the others.

This one was for John Gage, who was eighteen.

The visitor removed one of the tags from another gift that was for John and put it on the new one. The special one. With the pile of presents under the tree, and his own mother's handwriting on the tag, chances were good no one would take any notice of the strange new gift in the generic wrapper.

That was good.

For the Gages, and especially for the visitor—who now walked down the steps of the back porch and off into the woods behind the house—it was going to be a very different kind of holiday.

A blue Christmas, as Elvis sang. Elvis had no idea.

More like a red Christmas, the visitor thought, trotting along a path through the woods.

That's good. A red Christmas.

The ticking of the clock on the wall in the Lahiris' kitchen suddenly seemed terribly loud. Jenna stared at Priya for a few ticks, mouth open slightly in surprise.

"What do you mean, you quit?" she asked. "I mean, why?"

Priya smiled thinly. "Might have had something to do with the whole flunking-out-not-going-to-classes-semi-nervous-breakdown thing," she said, glancing away. "Figured I'd quit before they threw me out."

Jenna swallowed hard and reached out to take Priya's hand in both of her own. Her friend was in terrible pain, and Jenna could feel it radiating off her, could feel it creeping into her own body, forming ice around her heart.

"God, Pri, I'm so sorry," she said. "I wish you'd called me."

Priya shrugged. "No offense, but I don't know how much it would've helped. Plus, I don't know, I guess I

26

just thought that you and Moira would stay in touch, and I'd be left out in the cold."

"Why would you think that?" Jenna asked, horrified. "We were friends. Things were good over the summer, weren't they?"

"Yeah," Priya admitted. "But things were always different after Noah. Moira hated me for a while, and I figured you thought I was pretty much a jerk, too."

"I never thought that," Jenna said, surprised. "I didn't think it was the right thing to do, but we were always friends. We were always close. You could've called me."

Priya opened her mouth to reply, but nothing came out except a whimper. Her lower lip trembled and she started to cry. A second later, she threw her arms around Jenna and held on tight.

"I missed you so much," she sobbed.

Jenna held her friend and gently shushed her. "It's all right. I'm here now. You're one of my best friends, Priya. That'll always be true. Always."

For a fleeting moment Jenna felt guilty. Not that she was lying to Priya, but she had to wonder if her words were really true. Already, Yoshiko and Hunter were closer to her than any of her high school friends, and her boyfriend, Damon, was fast becoming her closest friend. But the love she felt in her heart for Priya overwhelmed such questions. Jenna offered what little comfort she could.

Several minutes went by as Priya calmed down and brought her emotions under control. Finally she pulled away from Jenna, sniffling, and reached for a napkin to wipe her nose.

"What a loser, huh?" she muttered.

"Don't be that way," Jenna told her. Then, after a pause, she asked the question. "What happened?"

Priya shook her head. "I don't know, really. I can't even understand it myself. The first couple of weeks, I was doing fine adjusting. But then I saw everyone making friends and hanging out together, and I realized I had nobody to talk to. The classes were so big; the professors seemed so far away . . . I just felt lonely.

"I stopped reading assignments. Started skipping a bunch of classes because I knew I wasn't prepared. When one of my professors called me on it, I kind of freaked out. I spent three days in the infirmary, ended up with a counselor. Not that it helped."

Priya paused, took a long breath, and then offered a slow, almost apologetic shrug.

"Then I came home."

"Wow. So, what now?" Jenna asked, a bit hesitantly.

"Nothing, for the moment," Priya revealed, obviously embarrassed at the admission. "I'm going to get a job. I'm not quitting, though. I want to spend a few months looking at other schools. Local schools, so I can be near my parents. Small schools. I really think I need that, just to be somewhere I don't feel so lost."

The girls sat together in silence for a bit, while Jenna tried to think of something to say. Eventually, Priya got up from the kitchen table to get Jenna more soda. While she was standing at the open refrigerator, Jenna glanced at the clock and saw that it was nearly noon.

"Hey," she said, trying to sound upbeat, "why don't we go out for lunch? My treat. We could hit Houlihan's."

"I don't think so, J. I haven't taken a shower or anything."

Jenna didn't miss a beat. "I'll wait."

Priya seemed almost annoyed. "Know what, Jenna? I really don't think I'm up to it. I'm glad you came by and everything. You don't know how glad. But I just don't—"

"Moira's having a party tonight. You're going."

Priya blinked, startled by Jenna's abruptness. With a frown, she ran a hand through her jet black hair, then brought her fingers, fluttering, up to her face, as if to hide.

"Don't do that," she said, pain on her face. "I'm dealing with my life. I don't need to be pushed."

Jenna got up from the table, expression both soft and resolute. She went over to Priya and bent down slightly to force the other girl to look up, to meet her gaze. For a second a fiery anger flared in Priya's eyes, a flush coming into her already dark features.

"Priya—"

"No," Priya said.

"Priya," Jenna repeated. "You said you don't need to be pushed. I think you do. Maybe Northwestern was overwhelming for you, but this isn't Northwestern. This is home. It's me, remember? It's us. Your friends. This is your town, your place. It won't seem right, having this party if you're not there."

The other girl only glared at her.

"If you don't come, I'll go to the party and get every single person there to get in their cars and come over here, and we'll have the party in your backyard instead."

Priya's stern expression broke, and she actually allowed herself a small smile.

"Have you been talking to my mother?" she demanded.

"Nope," Jenna promised. "But that doesn't mean I'm not going to start."

With a sigh, Priya rolled her eyes. "Lunch," she said. "We can go to lunch. The party, I don't know. We'll talk about it."

Jenna leaned back against the kitchen counter and smiled with relief. "Damn right we will," she said. "Go take a shower."

As she left the kitchen and headed upstairs to get ready, Priya scratched her head.

Trying to figure out how she got talked into this, Jenna thought. But she wasn't finished, either. If Jenna had to kidnap her, Priya would be going to Moira's party. *She has to. I can't let her just keep thinking she's alone.*

It was nearly one o'clock when Walter Slikowski pulled his van into the driveway in front of the house in Arlington where he had the first-floor apartment. There were only three steps in the front, and the owner of the home had been more than happy to construct a ramp for him. It was a lovely old Victorian house, and he had decorated his apartment meticulously. He spent little enough time there, so he wanted it to be a very pleasant place to come home to.

There were a great many books and several mirrors, with brass and oak to spare. He was also a great lover of plants. Then, of course, there was the stereo, which was really the heart of the place. There were compact discs everywhere, most of them jazz, and he often had complaints from his upstairs neighbor—the elderly mother of the landlord—that the music was too loud. It made him feel like a teenager when this happened, but that wasn't necessarily a bad thing.

It took him several minutes to get out of the van, moving from the driver's seat to the wheelchair, and then lowering himself on the hydraulic lift at the vehicle's side door. *A lot of trouble just to go to the post office*, he thought. But the trip couldn't have been avoided.

After Walter had informed the Somerset P.D. that Jim Kerchak had been murdered before he went off the roof of City Hall, they asked him to continue with the case as a consultant. Just before Christmas, he would normally have told them to forget it. But Kerchak had been a friend.

Walter had planned to spend the holidays with his brother Arthur's family in Irvington, New York, but that plan had to be scrapped. The brothers only saw each other at Christmas, save for the odd lucky happenstance, and Arthur had been frustrated by Walter's decision. But there was really no decision at all. He was staying.

Which was what had led him to the post office, where he had mailed the gifts he had bought for Arthur, his wife, Marianne, and their daughters, Anne and Heather. Confined to his wheelchair, Walter tried to avoid such minor road trips, preferring to do his errands en masse. But Christmas was Christmas.

Inside, he found his answering machine blinking

with a message from Arthur, reminding him that he was still welcome, even at the last minute. Walter sighed sadly. He'd make it up to Arthur, he promised himself. Perhaps sometime in January. Certainly by Valentine's Day. It wasn't as if he didn't have the vacation time saved up.

The soundtrack to *The Fabulous Baker Boys*, with its wonderful Dave Grusin tunes, was already in the CD player. Walter turned the music on, volume low, and wheeled his chair into the kitchen, where he put a pot of milk on to make himself a cup of hot cocoa.

While he waited for the milk to heat up, he went into the dining room and looked out the window at the backyard. It had begun to snow, though only very lightly, and a sprinkle of white now dotted the frozen grass and the little bit of woods behind the house.

Walter smiled. *A white Christmas.*

Somehow, that made things just the tiniest bit better.

His musings were interrupted by the doorbell. Quickly, he propelled himself into the kitchen and turned off the gas on the stove, then went through the living room to open the front door.

"Hello, Walter."

Natalie Kerchak, her red hair glistening with a scatter of melting snow, stood on the front stoop. Walter took a breath. Natalie had that effect on him and always had. In truth, he'd been half expecting her. If he hadn't been, her sudden appearance on his doorstep might have had him fumbling for words for several minutes.

"Natalie. Please, come in."

Walter moved back from the door to allow her to pass, then closed it behind her. Without waiting for any further invitation, Natalie went into the living room, and Walter turned to follow. There was an electricity about her that trailed in her wake. Or perhaps, he thought, it might have been between them.

"I'm so sorry about your brother," he said earnestly. "Jim was a good man, and a good friend."

Natalie put a hand to her forehead and took a moment, struggling to keep her composure. There was only the barest hint of tears in her eyes when she sat on the elegant loveseat, crossing her legs at the ankles.

"Thank you, Walter," she said, nodding. "You were always a good friend to him as well. To both of us."

Natalie paused, then glanced up at him, a melancholy smile playing at the edges of her lips. "It's awful to say this just now, I suppose, but it's good to see you, even now. You look well."

"Work keeps me young," he replied, a bit uncomfortably.

Natalie nodded. "Work was always what kept you going," she said a bit sadly. Then she chuckled. "Barbara sends her best."

"She and Jim made a wonderful couple," Slick replied. "How is she faring?"

With the tiniest arching of her eyebrows, Natalie told him all he needed to know about Barbara Kerchak's emotional state. Not that he was surprised. Her husband had been murdered. Of course she was a wreck.

Unless she did it, he thought, and then immediately cursed himself for even allowing such an idea into his head. He'd known the family twelve years, at least. Barbara Kerchak was no more capable of murder than he was himself. In any case, Jim's neck had been broken, and Barbara wouldn't have had the strength to do that.

"What are you thinking?" Natalie asked him suddenly.

Walter blushed a bit. "Just that you're right. I could never seem to get away from my work, could I?"

She ignored the question.

"The police told us you were consulting on Jim's murder," Natalie said. "Barbara asked me to come talk to you, see if you had any insight. It helps her to know you're involved."

Her eyes came up, her gaze searching his face. "It helps us both."

"I'm glad I can be of some comfort," he replied. "As for insight, I'm sorry to say I haven't had much of that just yet. I was at the scene, of course, but I didn't notice anything there that the police haven't already noted. As for the . . ."

His words trailed off. Slick cleared his throat, mentally backtracking. He was used to talking to the police or his colleagues about a case, not to the next of kin. Particularly not to someone who had once meant so much to him. The last thing he wanted was to seem callous, and so he picked his words carefully.

"Obviously, there were things about the condition of his body that made it clear his death was not an accident. Other than that, however, there's very little to go on at this point.

"I wish I had something more concrete to tell you."

Natalie took a long breath. Then she nodded and reached out for Walter's hand. Their fingers touched, briefly, reassuringly, and he felt a bittersweet shiver run through him.

Once upon a time, he thought.

As if she'd read his mind, Natalie smiled. Then, a second later, she rose from the sofa. Walter glanced up at her, and for a moment he was back in time, back in that brief, perfect year during which he had loved her. He had never been a man who could easily open himself up to others, but from Natalie, he hid nothing. When they were together.

When he wasn't at work, or thinking about work, or living and breathing work.

"Thanks for talking to me," she said, as though he had saved her life. "Will you let us know if there are any developments?"

"Of course I will," Walter reassured her.

Natalie walked to the door, and he propelled himself after her. As she walked out onto the stoop and turned to smile sadly at him again, Walter saw that the snow was falling harder now and a light dusting covered the entire world beyond his door with a sparkling veil of white, as though the moment had been preserved for eternity.

The snow fell all around her, but Natalie didn't even seem to notice.

Walter wanted to say something, thought he *must* say something. It had been six years, after all, since he had last seen her, save for one time, driving his van along Tremont Street in Boston.

Suddenly her smile disappeared. The moment had passed. Natalie's face revealed a grave burden she had not spoken of before. Clearly, she was troubled by something more than her brother's murder.

"What is it?" he asked.

"The police are going to assume that if it isn't domestic, it must be political," Natalie replied.

"Naturally. He was the mayor."

"They asked Barbara and me if he had any enemies, if we thought there was anyone who hated him enough to do this. We told them no."

Now Walter was troubled. "And?"

Natalie gazed at him intently, intimately. "Walter, you've known Jim for years. He was a good man. He would never hurt anybody, but that doesn't mean he was a saint, either. If he thought no one would know, and nobody would be hurt, I can't say if he wouldn't have—"

She broke off then, and her features collapsed into an expression of pain and sorrow, tears springing to her eyes. She wiped them off, straightened up, and pulled herself together.

"I don't know what to say," Walter confessed helplessly.

"Politicians routinely take money in exchange for their influence," Natalie said defensively. "It happens every day. I don't think Jim would have done something like that, but if you find out otherwise, I was just hoping you'd tell Barbara and me before we heard it on the news."

"Of course I will," he promised.

She nodded, then turned and strode down the ramp in front of the house, slipping a bit on the snowy surface. Walter called after her, but Natalie didn't turn until she was already at her car. Wiping tears from her eyes, she raised a hand as if to brush him away.

"I'm all right," she said. "I'll be all right. I know you'll do what you can."

Natalie got into her car, started it up, and pulled out of the driveway almost without looking. She was nearly broadsided by a minivan. Then, a moment later, she was gone, leaving Walter sitting in his wheelchair in the open doorway watching the snow fall.

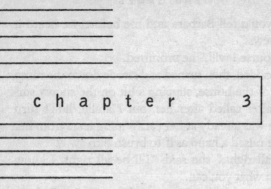

chapter 3

By the time Jenna got home that afternoon, it was past four o'clock. The snow was falling steadily, though slowly: fat, heavy flakes that shrouded the sky and built up on the lawns and trees, the frosting on what looked to be a perfect Christmas.

As promised, her mother was in the kitchen, beginning the long process that would end with Louisiana chicken and dumplings, one of Jenna's favorite meals. The spicy stew wasn't, as April noted, exactly Christmasy, but neither of them minded.

Jenna loaded the five-disc changer with various holiday albums, everything from Sinatra to Harry Connick, Jr., to *A Very Special Christmas*. The Blake women sang along to every tune as Jenna pitched in, cutting vegetables and mixing the batter for the dumplings.

"Eggnog?" April asked as she pulled the chicken from the bone.

"With or without alcohol?" Jenna asked, one eyebrow raised.

April grinned. "Without, young lady. You're driving."

"I know. Just checking. There is cinnamon, though, right?"

"And nutmeg. I know our official indulgence together isn't until tomorrow night, but I figured eggnog was always welcome."

Jenna couldn't have agreed more. It was Christmas Eve, after all.

When the huge pot was finally simmering on the stove, Jenna and her mother went into the living room to settle in front of the TV with big cups of eggnog. As Jenna flipped channels, she ran across a news report about the death of Somerset's mayor. It was finally confirmed that Jim Kerchak had been murdered, and police were looking for help from the community, hoping that anyone with any information, or anyone who had seen anything out of the ordinary the night of the murder, would come forward.

"That's just so awful," April said.

"Yeah. Merry Christmas," Jenna replied cynically. "I wonder if anyone ever actually calls in with useful information."

The channel surfing went on, and they found Patrick Stewart playing Scrooge on TNT. As they settled in to watch the ghost of Jacob Marley do some haunting, Jenna's mind went back to Mayor Kerchak's murder and autopsy. And to Slick. Just before she'd left, he told her he had canceled his visit to see his brother for the holidays. More than likely, he was at home, doing nothing, by himself on Christmas Eve.

With a small smile, Jenna stood up from the couch. "I'll be right back," she told her mother.

Upstairs in her bedroom, she rooted around in the suitcase she'd brought home and hardly unpacked to find her address book. Just a couple of weeks earlier, she had finally written Dr. Slikowski's home number into her book, just in case.

He answered on the third ring.

"Dr. Slikowski, it's Jenna."

"Jenna," he said, concern creeping into his voice. "What is it? Has something happened?"

She chuckled. "No. Nothing like that. I knew you weren't going away, and I just thought I'd call to say 'Merry Christmas.' "

"Jenna," he said, sounding touched. "That's very sweet. Merry Christmas to you and your mother, as well."

"Thanks. So, any progress?"

Slick fell silent. Jenna hoped she didn't sound insensitive. She certainly hadn't meant to. It was simply that she knew he was working on the case, and it would be bothering him now that the world was about to take a station break, closing down for Christmas. For at least twenty-four hours, there'd be nothing he could do.

"Not really," he said finally. "Or at least, nothing substantial. Of course, the mind tends to create motives out of thin air. Political figures tend to be murdered for one of several reasons: to make a statement, to keep them silent, or to get them out of the way because they stand in the way of somebody illegally making a lot of money."

"Aren't most good politicians in the way of somebody making a lot of money illegally?" Jenna asked.

Again, Slick paused. It bothered her. Normally, he would have agreed with her, and she had to wonder what there was about her statement that he didn't agree with.

Unless Jim Kerchak wasn't *a good politician.*

Perturbed by that thought, she was too preoccupied to hear the first few words as Slick started to speak again.

"I'm sorry?" she said. "What was that?"

Which was when Dr. Slikowski proceeded to tell Jenna about the visit he had received from Natalie Kerchak, sister of the late mayor, and obviously an old friend. Jenna was fascinated. This was more about Slick's personal life—even, as in this case, implied personal life—than he had ever revealed before.

"I'm in this thing up to my neck," he said with a dry laugh. "I want to know who did this because Jim was my friend, but now I have other people who are counting on me to help figure it out."

"Well, you *are* in a position to get pretty deeply into this case if you want to. You'll figure it out."

"I wish I was as sure about that as you are," he replied. "So far, we've got nothing. Whoever did it was strong enough to break Jim's neck, and strong enough to throw—rather than push—him from the roof of City Hall."

"How do you know that?" Jenna asked, intrigued.

"Trajectory," Slick explained. "If he'd fallen off, or even been pushed, he would have landed closer to the building. No, he was thrown. Thing is, there isn't a single sign of a struggle up there, or any other clue as to what went on."

He started to say something else, but Jenna interrupted him. "How do you know what the roof looked like? I can't imagine there's an elevator that goes up there."

"There isn't," he confirmed. "But the police photographer took plenty of shots."

"I can't imagine that gives you the whole picture."

"You're right about that," he admitted, though his voice had become tight, a bit defensive. "But that's the primary limitation of being in a wheelchair, Jenna. You can't go everywhere."

Jenna felt self-conscious, as she always did on those rare occasions when Slick discussed his disability. She almost felt as though she ought to apologize, but before she could, Dr. Slikowski went on.

"I'm glad you said that, though," he told her. "If I am going to try to get more involved with this case, from a forensic perspective, I need to get a look at that roof."

"Isn't it too late, though, with the snow?"

"Maybe. Maybe not. I know you're on vacation, but how would you feel about lending me a hand, day after tomorrow?"

"Sure," Jenna agreed. *At this point, I can't exactly bail on him, especially since I was the one who brought it up.*

"Excellent. I'll ask Audrey Gaines to make sure only the police have access to the roof in the meantime. I'll speak to you on the twenty-sixth, then."

"Okay," Jenna said. "Merry Christmas."

"To you, too. And Jenna?"

"Yes?"

"It really was kind of you to call."

After she hung up, Jenna marveled, certainly not for the first time, at the strangeness of her life. The things she found herself involved in were things that kids her age were only supposed to see on the news. In a short while, she would be reunited with a lot of her friends from high school, people to whom the world she lived in now would seem not only foreign, but peculiar, even terrifying.

In an odd way, the thought made her very proud. Which, she knew, probably had a great deal to do with a fact of her life that she was only truly beginning to understand.

Slick needed her.

Jenna thought that was very cool.

It was tradition at Chris Meserve's house that after dinner on Christmas Eve, each member of the family was allowed to open one gift. They sat around the living room, content after the seafood feast Mrs. Meserve always made Christmas Eve as a nod to the Sicilian traditions in which she had been raised. They all grabbed the first thing they found with their name on it.

43

Never something big, though. That was the only rule. The big things were always held back until the following morning.

That particular Christmas Eve, Mr. Meserve found himself the proud owner of a new electric screwdriver, which he had been dropping hints about for months. His old one had burned out its motor, and he always liked using the thing, rather than doing all that tedious twisting by hand.

Mrs. Meserve was not quite so happy. Though she was certain her family had provided a few surprises for her under the tree—which together they had lovingly decorated with ornaments and lights and tinsel, and the angel her great-grandmother had made by hand—the present she opened was a pair of black kid leather gloves. They were lovely, to be sure, but Mrs. Meserve had picked them out herself and told her husband just where to buy them. It was the one gift she'd known she would be receiving.

Their daughter, Allison, who was just fourteen, was ecstatic when she tore the colorful Santa paper off the portable CD player with headphones that had been number one on her Christmas wish list.

All three of them were, therefore, quite distracted—Dad and Allison with opening and examining their gifts, Mom with putting a pot of coffee on to go with dessert—so that nobody was paying attention while Chris opened his gift, a small, rectangular package wrapped in plain green paper.

"Huh," Chris grunted, wondering what to make of his gift, and who had bought it for him.

Curious, he went down the hall to his room to try it out.

Chris didn't have much time, though. In a little while, he had to head out for Moira Kearney's party.

He knew it was going to be a blast.

After dinner Jenna used her mother's computer to pick up her e-mail. There were only two messages. One was a general memo from Somerset about when students would be allowed back on campus, and the process for requesting early readmission to the dorms. Apparently there had already been a lot of such requests, and most students had only been away from the university for a few days.

But Jenna read the other message first. It was from Yoshiko. Jenna smiled the moment she saw the subject line: "How's the Arctic?"

> Hey J!
>
> Hope you're having fun in the Great White North. It was eighty here today. Perfect for surfing and lazing about on the sand. :) Not to rub it in or anything. We're having all the relatives here for Christmas dinner. And, no, it's not going to be a luau! The day after tomorrow, Mom and I are going shopping in Honolulu, and later in the week, we're all going to Kauai for a little expedition. The waterfalls and wildflowers make it like a little paradise. I'll bring back pictures.
>
> Okay, just in case I've been faking it well, much as I missed my family, I'm already looking forward

to going back to school. I've talked to Hunter. He sounds sad. Call him if you can. I miss you both so much.

Merry Christmas, Jenna.

Love you,

Yoshiko

Jenna wrote back immediately.

Uh-huh. First of all, Kitsuta, you DO NOT surf. Liar.

Other than that, yes, I'm incredibly jealous. We should think about spring break in Hawaii, don't you think? Unless you don't want to go home for what's supposed to be a wild party.

Mom and I are going to my uncle's for Christmas dinner. I got home late--tied up with something for Slick--but I'm off to a party with some friends right now. Haven't been able to talk to Damon much, but I will. Sigh. He'll be in Florida, you'll be in Hawaii, Hunter's in Louisiana . . . and I'm freezing my ass off. On the other hand, I wouldn't be anywhere else for Christmas.

Guess what? It's snowing. That's how it's supposed to be. Santa drives a sleigh, honey. You're lucky he even makes it out your way.

I'll try to call Hunter tomorrow. I miss you guys, too.

LYKYAMY,

Jenna

On the way to Moira's house, Jenna stopped to pick up Priya. It was snowing a bit more heavily than it had been earlier, so she went slow and was particularly careful taking corners or braking before an intersection. Jenna knew Noah, and most of the other guys, would have given her a hard time for "driving like a granny." She didn't care. Once upon a time she had been in the car with Noah when he tried to show off, purposely fishtailing on a snowy street.

The car had ended up door-handle deep in a snow bank. Noah probably hadn't learned a lesson that day, but Jenna certainly had.

Fat white flakes swept down from the sky. In the dome of light thrown by each street lamp, Jenna could see just how heavy the snowfall had become. It was beautiful. There were already several inches on the ground, enough to make it a white Christmas.

Okay, you can stop now, she thought.

Cautious as ever, she turned into Priya's steep driveway, headlights illuminating the falling snow. Jenna beeped, and a minute later, she saw Priya, jacket hood up, making her way along the path from the front door, then down the slate stairs to the driveway.

The girl who got into the passenger seat looked nothing like the girl who had met her at the door that morning, nor even the girl she had gone to lunch with that afternoon. *This* was the Priya she knew: elegant red jacket with hood, off-white turtleneck, black slacks, black leather boots with just a hint of a heel.

Jenna grinned at her. "You know you're going to fall on your ass in those boots?"

Priya arched an eyebrow. "We'll see."

There was humor there, but something else as well. Jenna knew exactly what it was: fear. Priya had always been fashionable—she just had style—and this outfit wasn't all that unusual for her wardrobe. But Jenna couldn't shake the idea that it was akin to wearing a mask to hide her face, her identity.

Then again, if that's what she needs right now, what's the harm? At least she's going.

Jenna sighed. "Of course, looking at you, I now feel totally underdressed."

"Like it's the first time?" Priya teased.

Jenna whacked her on the arm. Then they were off, headed over to Moira's, which was several miles away.

It was just after eight when they pulled down the long drive in front of the Kearneys', an old New England farmhouse with a rambling front porch and about four acres of property all around it. Moira's father had wanted to sell two or three building lots a few years earlier, but Mrs. Kearney put her foot down. They agreed not to talk about it again until their youngest—fifteen-year-old Julie—was in college. And even then, she knew she would still hate the idea. Once, the property had been the core of a real, working farm. They even had the barn to prove it. But now it was just a nice little corner of the world, with trees and a hill and a little brook that ran through one edge of the property.

It was almost like living in the country, only it was Natick, a standard-bearer for middle-class, suburban, mall-trained America.

The Kearneys had money, obviously. Moira's father was an expensive attorney whose office was in Boston. Still, in spite of the private and Catholic schools in the area, the Kearneys believed in the public education system. Jenna was happy about that. If Moira had gone to Catholic school, they might never have met.

There were nearly a dozen cars scattered up and down the Kearneys' long driveway, many of them pulled partially onto the lawn. Though a lot of parents would freak if anybody parked on their lawn, it was expected at the Kearneys'. They had a big family, a lot of gatherings, which fed into the whole farmhouse atmosphere.

Jenna parked her dad's car and got out. Priya followed, hair shielded from the snow by her hood, tiny face lost in its folds. They didn't even glance at the main house, but instead walked past it across the deepening snow to the barn beyond. Lights glowed in the windows of the huge structure, and music blared from within. The Kearneys' barn wasn't heated, but they'd had winter parties there in the past, and with a couple of space heaters and a lot of dancing, nobody ever seemed to mind. *Well, except that one time my nostrils froze,* Jenna remembered.

Then she blocked it out. Unhappy memory.

A moment before they reached the two huge doors, one of them was pushed outward, and two guys came out into the dark and the snow. The light from inside caused her to blink as the guys walked past, and it took Jenna a moment to realize one of the them was

Chris Meserve, who'd been a friend of hers at Natick High. Not that they'd been that close, but certainly, they knew each other pretty well.

"Hey, Chris," she said amiably, tapping him as he passed. "What happened? One semester of college and you're a snob now?"

The guys both turned to look at Priya and Jenna, appraising them in that *guy* way. But Jenna could see from the way Chris looked at her, with a question in his eyes, that he didn't recognize her. She was surprised. It wasn't as though she had changed that much. Her hair was a bit longer, that was true, but it was the same color. She weighed, she thought, maybe ten pounds more than she had in high school, but it wasn't as if she had gotten fat. She was about to say something when recognition lit up Chris's face, and he grinned.

"Jenna, wow!" he said admiringly. "You look so different. Sorry, I didn't really recognize you at first."

"Different how?" she asked, a little on the defensive.

"In a good way," he promised. "College life has been good to you, huh?"

Jenna smiled. Nodded.

"We'll see you back in there in a second," Chris informed her. "Just answering the call of nature."

"Great," Jenna replied sarcastically. "Thanks for sharing."

They were about to go inside when Chris glanced at Priya.

"Wait. Priya, right?" he asked. When she nodded, he laughed. "Well, all right. You look amazing."

"Thanks," she replied. Then she glanced at the other guy, the tall, thin guy standing next to Chris. "Hey, Ben."

The guy smiled, seemed flattered that Priya had remembered him. "Hey, Priya. Good to see you. Maybe we can catch up inside?"

"I'd like that," Priya said.

Then Chris and Ben were going around behind the barn, where the woods began. The girls went through the door, and Jenna turned to close it behind her.

"Who was that guy?" she asked.

Priya frowned. "Ben Keough. You don't remember him? He was my bio partner, freshman year."

For a moment Jenna couldn't place the nice-looking, soft-spoken guy. Then suddenly, a broad grin spread across her face.

"Wait, wait, is this the guy who gave you the note after graduation? How he had a crush on you for four years and couldn't get up the guts to ask you out?"

Priya smiled shyly. "That's him," she confessed.

"See, this is already a good party," Jenna told her.

The girls chuckled, then waded in among the dozens of people gathered in the barn. There were coolers of beer all around, not to mention the pizza boxes and bags of chips and such on makeshift tables. There were stalls on either side of the barn, and most of them were filled with old junk from the days when the Kearney place was still a farm. Several had been cleaned out, however, and there were chairs in there. A big cardboard No Smoking sign hung on the far wall.

Good idea, Jenna thought. There wasn't any hay or anything in the barn, but she figured the old timber was dry as kindling. Even the three small space heaters were propped up on top of old metal construction barrels that had somehow found their way into the barn years earlier.

On the single real table, a relatively new-looking picnic thing with attached benches, there were two large green coffee pots plugged into long orange power cables. If past experience was any indication, Jenna knew she'd find coffee in one of them, but the other would be the real score—hot apple cider with cinnamon, homemade by Moira's mom.

Though they set out for the table, Jenna's mind on that hot cider, they hadn't made it half a foot before they started to run into their old classmates. Carol Helfer, Julianna Guarino, Joey Bausch, Tomas Garza. Jenna and Priya were both overwhelmed to see so many old friends, the nostalgia, the catching up.

From time to time Jenna glanced over at Priya, worried that the constant questions—not to mention everyone's stories about how wonderful things were going for them at college—would bring her down. She needn't have worried. Whatever she was telling—or not telling—people about her situation, Priya looked very happy, very comfortable, just to be in such a familiar setting. Jenna was profoundly relieved.

Finally, twenty minutes after they'd walked in, the two girls made it to the table with the coffee and cider. As they served themselves large cups of the hot apple concoction, garnished with cinnamon sticks for stirring, Jenna took a long breath. She missed college, missed her friends, and missed her boyfriend, Damon, most of all. But this little reunion was something she had sorely needed.

On the other hand, the person she most wanted to see, the hostess, seemed to be M.I.A.

"I wonder where Moira is," she told Priya.

"You looking for Moira?" a voice said.

Jenna turned to see yet another familiar face. She grinned. "John! How are you?"

For several minutes she caught up with John Gage. They'd gone on a few dates sophomore year, but nothing had ever come of it. Still, she'd always liked him. A genuinely nice guy, but way too into sports for her. He had scruffy black hair and a light spatter of freckles over the bridge of his nose that some girls, herself included, found sexy. Others thought it made him look like a little kid. Although Jenna doubted those girls would say the same these days. More so than most of the people she'd caught up with, John Gage looked different, older. Even the shape of his face had changed.

It was a good change.

Good thing I have a boyfriend, she thought, *or I might say something I'd regret later.*

"So, *have* you seen Moira?" she asked.

"Yeah. She's in the stall over there," he said, and pointed. "Catching up on old times with Noah, I think."

"Thanks," Jenna replied. But inside, her response

was a very serious *uh-oh*. If Moira and Noah were getting together, it might have been a bad idea to bring Priya after all.

As John moved away, Jenna turned and nearly bumped into Priya, who had a cynical little smile on her face.

"You heard?" Jenna asked, though she knew the answer. "Are you okay?"

Priya thought about it, as though she wasn't quite sure of the answer. After a bit, she nodded. "Noah was with Moira a lot longer than he was with me," she said. "She goes to school three thousand miles away. Life goes on, right?"

"That's what I've been telling you," Jenna replied.

They went in search of Moira. Just as John had predicted, they found her in a stall near the barn doors, sitting on a metal folding chair, leaning back as she talked to Noah. In mid-sentence, she glanced up to see Jenna and Priya coming her way.

Moira shrieked at the top of her lungs, her face nearly split in two by her smile. Jenna laughed as her friend rushed to her and pulled her into a crushing embrace that nearly knocked the wind out of her.

"Oh, my God! You look totally phenomenal!" Moira cried.

Then she grabbed Priya in a hug that was just as strong. Priya coughed, pretending that she couldn't breathe, and Moira let go, only to chide her and give her a light punch to the shoulder.

"Wow, do I feel neglected," Noah put in, feigning sadness.

All three of them attacked him with punches, growling. Noah just laughed, blue eyes sparkling. It was old shtick, but somehow, it broke the ice. Whatever was going on in their lives, it wasn't more important than the bond they shared.

"So, you two looked pretty cozy in here," Jenna said, one eyebrow raised in accusation.

"Hey," Noah said, hands up in defense. "I have a girlfriend. Don't go spreading rumors."

"From what I've heard, Mr. Levine, you have lots of girlfriends," Priya teased.

Jenna and Moira roared. Noah looked frustrated.

"Where did you hear that?" he asked.

"I have friends at UMass, don't you worry," Priya told him. "A nice little network of spies to pass on the latest gossip about your behavior to my buds."

The girls all grinned, and soon enough, the four of them were laughing and talking, just catching up. Jenna thought Moira had never looked so good, her blond hair falling in ringlets to her shoulders. Priya told Moira and Noah what had been happening with her, and that led to a few minutes of grave talk about school. All of them, it seemed, had had their problems. Jenna was a bit coy when discussing her own— she didn't want to freak them all out by telling them of her brushes with violence. But she thought the conversation was healthy for Priya; it would be helpful for her to realize that none of them thought college was paradise.

Though Jenna noticed that Moira seemed to be taking to the L.A. lifestyle. She had already acted in a few student films, though her real desire was to write screenplays.

"Still, though, if I can do a little acting, too, I sure wouldn't mind," she told them.

"Of course, you'd have to get implants," Noah said.

He looked dead serious, but when all three of them went to hit him simultaneously, he cracked up.

In the midst of their laughter, they were interrupted by Kyleigh Dervin, who poked her head into the stall.

"Hey, Moi, you better get out here," she said anxiously.

"What's wrong?" Moira asked, immediately starting toward Kyleigh.

"Maybe it's none of my business," Kyleigh said—though it was very clear to Jenna that she didn't mean the words at all—"but your little sister went for a walk with Tomas Garza. They were both pretty drunk."

"Damn," Moira muttered, and started for the barn doors. "Any idea which way they went?"

While Kyleigh was pointing toward the apple trees way back behind the main house, Noah looked over at Jenna and Priya.

"What the hell's wrong with him? Tommy's gotta know she's only fifteen."

"Your point would be what?" Priya said, her tone more cynical than usual. "He's a guy. She's cute and drunk and young enough to think he's fascinating."

The four of them spent the next fifteen minutes calling out for Julie Kearney. When she came tromping out of the woods, tucking in her shirt, she was far more angry than embarrassed.

Fifteen, Jenna mused. *At fifteen, we're all just ticking bombs.*

Tomas walked out a moment later. Noah stepped forward and started to give the other guy a hard time. He barely got the chance. Moira, Priya, and Jenna gave the guy a severely humiliating tongue-lashing and sent him back to the barn with his tail between his legs. Julie was drunk—another thing Kyleigh had been right about—and Moira threatened to tell their parents unless her sister went to bed right then.

Sulkily, cursing Moira the whole way, Julie slouched off toward the house.

It was quite a party.

A little after midnight Chris Meserve stumbled into his house, a little buzzed from the hot cider he'd tipped Southern Comfort into. His family was asleep—Mom, Dad, and Allison—and the spectacle of Christmas morning was just seven or eight hours away.

Before he went to sleep, though, he wanted to check out the early Christmas present he had opened after dinner.

A short time later he began to shudder uncontrollably. He clenched his fists so tightly that his fingernails sliced into his palms. His muscles spasmed as his body convulsed, and he nearly choked to death on his tongue.

When the convulsions stopped, with eyes wide and bloodshot, and lips pulled back in a grotesque expression that was definitely not a smile, Chris went into the kitchen, pulled a huge knife from the butcher block, and slaughtered his entire family as they slept.

c h a p t e r 4

On Christmas morning, all was silent. The world was blue and white. The snow had stopped falling sometime during the night, and the sky was clear. Sunlight glinted off the topmost layer, quickly hardened to a frozen crust, and that icy sheen sparkled. No cars passed by on the road outside, not that early in the morning. For the most part, phones did not ring, televisions remained dark, stereos played only the music of the season. Alarms were unnecessary, either because there was no rush to rise and face the day or because the thrill of it had already done the job.

In her bed, under a white goose-down comforter, with a stuffed Winnie-the-Pooh unconsciously clutched against her, Jenna Blake slept soundly, sweetly. Throughout the night, her room had been lit with the warm orange light of the electric candles her mother always put in the windows. The bulbs were still burning that morning, though their light was diffused against the sunshine outside. Beyond her window, though, the white-dappled trees in the yard offered the perfect backdrop.

Christmas morning.

When she was very small, Jenna would rise from bed and toddle into her parents' room, asking so softly if today was the day. If Santa had come. Exhausted— up too late, awakened too early—her parents would grin broadly and walk her downstairs to the living room, where the Christmas tree would be surrounded by presents, and by the little fence that prevented her from pulling ornaments down or yanking on the strands of lights.

Jenna barely remembered those Christmas mornings before the family had fallen apart, before Christmas had become strictly a girls' celebration. But she dreamed about them.

To her, Christmas was a whirlwind. She would jump out of bed, run into her mother's room and pounce, waking her mother just enough so that the groggy woman could stumble down the stairs after her. They'd have French toast together, and greasy bacon, and hot chocolate made with Quik. That was absolutely necessary. Once, April had tried to make the real thing, with milk and actual chocolate, and Jenna had fumed. Quik was what she wanted.

There would always be a few gifts for April. Sometimes things "Santa" had brought for her, and later, things that Jenna had picked out and that her mother had paid for. In eighth grade, Jenna finally started buying her mother's presents with her own money. She loved that part. Surprising her mother was a thrill for her.

And always, always, always, Jenna was up before her mother.

Until now.

Burrowed deep within the sanctuary of her comforter and pillows and Pooh bear, Jenna stirred, frowning as she became aware of the world around her. Her eyes were barely slits, yet the first things she saw were the orange-bulbed electric candles in the windows. Somewhere close by, Nat King Cole sang "The Christmas Song," and someone sang along. A small smile crept across Jenna's sleepy face.

"You really should let Nat handle the vocals," she rasped, stretching, groaning as she came fully awake.

At the door to her room, her mother stood and sang, ignoring Jenna's criticism. She paused long enough to sip from a steaming mug of something good, then set the mug down on Jenna's bureau and moved, smiling, to Jenna's bedside.

"Aaahh!" Jenna cried, sticking her fingers in her ears.

Her mother grabbed her by the arms, pulled her up out of bed, and dragged her in a stumbling dance. Jenna started laughing and, at last, joined in the singing.

When the song ended, they giggled together.

"You are such a complete and total goofball," Jenna told her.

"Merry Christmas, honey," April replied, and kissed her daughter on the forehead.

Jenna hugged her mother and returned the sentiment.

"You must have been up pretty late last night," April chided. "Good party, was it?"

"Not bad," Jenna told her. "Priya definitely seems better."

"That's good," her mother said idly. "Although it's a shame you slept late. You know what happens when you sleep in on Christmas morning."

Jenna narrowed her eyes in suspicion. "No. What happens?"

April shrugged. "Santa returns all the presents to the mall."

With a look of absolute horror, Jenna put her hands on her hips. "I don't think so!" she cried. Then she bolted out of the room and down the hall, scrambling down the steps as April gave chase.

In the living room she came to a quick halt in front of the Christmas tree, surprised to see how many colorfully wrapped boxes there were. April had obviously put more out that morning. Jenna turned around to see her mother come into the room.

"Hey," she said. "Am I missing something? Do I have a long-lost brother or sister who's joining us?" Jenna was thoughtful, then her eyes widened as she thought of her half brother in the Marine Corps. "Is Pierce coming?"

"No," her mother replied. "I just missed you while you were at school. Plus, I figured you could use all the help you could get. Not to mention that, with the house empty, and not having to clean up after my sloppy daughter, I had more time to shop."

Jenna didn't even register the barb. She glanced down guiltily.

"I only got you one thing."

April frowned. "I'm the mom. It's my prerogative to spoil you at Christmas. And whatever you got me, I'm sure I'll love it because it's from you. As long as you never have a secretary or assistant go out and buy my Christmas gifts, I'll be a happy mother."

Jenna chuckled. "Still, Mom, you spent a lot of money . . ."

"How do you know?" April retorted. "It could be all stuff from the One Dollar store. Hey, don't forget your stocking."

Above a fireplace that had gone unused for at least a decade, a green-and-red stocking made of heavy wool hung from the mantel. The letters of Jenna's name had been cut out in two-inch-high pieces of felt. The stocking had been handmade not long after Jenna was born. Every year it was filled with pretty much the same array of things her mother picked up the week before Christmas: perfume, candy canes, chocolate Santas, deodorant and other toiletries. As holiday moments went, dumping the stocking wasn't exactly glamorous. And yet, in some ways, it meant just as much to Jenna as any other part of Christmas.

With a grin, she went over to the fireplace, plopped down cross-legged on the floor, and upended the contents of her stocking on the floor. The usual stash spilled onto the carpet. Holiday-wrapped Hershey's Kisses were a new and very welcome addition.

Jenna frowned as she spotted a small box, wrapped

in silver foil paper, which had been at the bottom of the stocking and was now atop the heap.

"What's this?"

"A little something from your father."

There was something in her mother's voice that Jenna couldn't quite interpret. She turned to examine April's face, but her expression was unreadable. It wasn't what she would have expected, however. It wasn't bitterness. Her parents weren't exactly the best of friends. In fact, they never even spoke unless it had something to do with Jenna. In the past, Christmas gifts from her father—usually too-small sweaters or Barbies (something she'd grown out of at the age of seven)—brought only a dubiously raised eyebrow from her mother.

Jenna unwrapped the box, then halted in surprise when she saw the imprint on the cover: Barmakian Brothers Jewelers. Again, she glanced back at her mother.

April smiled. "It's really from both him and Shayna. Your father's going to miss you while they're in France. He wanted you to know."

Jenna flipped open the top of the box, and took a quick, sudden breath. Inside was a diamond-and-amethyst bracelet. She stared at it for a long moment.

Then she started to cry. Softly at first, and then great, heaving sobs.

"Hey, hey," her mother whispered, kneeling at her side and pulling Jenna into an embrace. "He can be a real jerk sometimes, but I'm sure tears weren't the desired response."

It was a minute before she could speak. Finally she smiled and wiped away the tears.

"It's stupid," Jenna said, voice hitching with emotion. "Really stupid. I mean, I'm sure Shayna picked it out and all. But it's just . . ." Jenna sobbed again. When she continued, it was through her tears. "This is the first time in my whole life . . . and I mean my *whole* life . . . that I ever felt like he bought something for *me*. That he actually put some thought into it. That it mattered to him."

When she managed to meet her mother's gaze again, she saw that now there were tears in April's eyes, too.

"He missed a lot, Jenna. You both did. I think maybe he's just now starting to realize how much he lost by not being there for you," her mother said. "Now he's finally starting to act like a human being, finally doing the right thing, and he goes and leaves for France."

Jenna grinned. "Maybe his timing is right. After all, it could only go downhill from here, right?"

They laughed together, and then just sat, not speaking, taking in the beauty of Nat King Cole's perfect voice.

"All right," April said after a bit. "Open your presents. I'm sure it'll all be anticlimactic now, though. Your father stole my thunder."

Which wasn't true at all. Jenna's mother had gone a little crazy that Christmas. There were handcrafted leather boots, and an ankle-length brown leather coat that was too sexy for words.

"My baby's all grown up," April said when Jenna opened that one. "You might as well look the part."

There were books she had asked for, and discs she hadn't. Her mother liked to introduce her to new types of music at Christmas, surprising Jenna with things she'd either never heard or wouldn't have thought of listening to if they hadn't been gifts. Most of the time, Jenna found she enjoyed those CDs more than the ones she bought for herself. There were more books and what amounted to a wild shopping spree's worth of clothes, all but one sweater of which Jenna loved. The sweater was mustard colored.

Nasty.

There were even more books, and two pairs of shoes from Nine West, and a heavy gold anklet that was another surprise. There was an antique Chinese puzzle box that Jenna practically danced with joy over.

There was an ancient hardcover copy of *The Maltese Falcon*, signed by Dashiell Hammett.

Jenna stared at the signature. Then at her mother. Then back at the signature. She ran her fingers lightly over the paper, just below the author's signature.

"Is this real?" she whispered.

April laughed. "Of course it's real."

"Where did you get it?"

"I have friends. One of them collects rare books. He let me pay in installments. Lots of installments."

Jenna held the book against her flannel pajama top and went over to hug her mother, trapping the expensive volume between them.

"Thank you so much, Mom. This is amazing."

"Well," April replied oh-so-matter-of-factly, "I couldn't let your father show me up, now could I?"

Jenna laughed, and held her even more tightly. She blinked suddenly and stood back.

"Oh. I never even put your present under the tree," she said, alarmed. Then she grinned. "I did manage to get it wrapped, though."

Placing the book on the coffee table, Jenna dashed upstairs to her room and came back down a moment later with a box wrapped in Frosty the Snowman paper. After all that her mother had done for her, Jenna felt as though her gift was horribly insignificant.

However, the look on April's face when she unwrapped it changed all that. It was an antique perfume bottle, purple and blue and red hand-blown glass, with the most delicate design Jenna had ever seen.

"It's beautiful, Jenna," her mother said. "Thank you so much."

Nat gave way to Frank, who gave way to Bing, who gave way to Harry Connick and eventually, to her mother's dismay, to Mariah Carey; though April had to admit that Mariah's Christmas album was pretty spectacular. They made their way through French toast, with the requisite hot chocolate. By the time they were showered and dressed and ready to go to Uncle Brian's, it was eleven-thirty.

The entire ride to her uncle's house, Jenna and her mother talked about everything under the sun, the two of them sharing the way they always used to, but hadn't really had a chance to do since Jenna had gone to college in September. When they got to the subject of Damon, however, Jenna freaked. She had meant to call him, to wish him a merry Christmas, but had forgotten, and he and his family were flying to Captiva Island in Florida the next day.

"Don't worry," her mother told her. "You can call him when you get home. It can't be that much of an emergency. He didn't call *you* this morning either."

Jenna couldn't argue with that logic. But thinking about it did put the slightest taint on what had otherwise been the perfect Christmas morning.

Walter had woken at seven, a mere half hour later than he did every other morning. The process of bathing and dressing was an arduous one, in spite of the apparatuses all about the house meant to aid him in such things. By eight, he had settled himself in for a breakfast of scrambled eggs and wheat toast with jelly, and a tall glass of pulpy orange juice.

At nine o'clock, as if it were chiming the hour, his phone began to ring. Walter smiled at the sound, presuming that it was his brother, calling to say how much they all missed him and wished he were there to celebrate the day.

He answered the phone. "Merry Christmas."

"My, you sound cheerful. I guess I can't call you Ebenezer after all."

The sweet, laughing voice belonged to Natalie Kerchak. Part of him wondered how genuine her pleasantry was, considering her brother's murder, but he knew it would be in truly bad form to call her on it. If she had to force it a bit to feel happy, he certainly wasn't going to steal that from her.

"Natalie. What a nice surprise for Christmas morning."

"You're listening to that GRP Records jazz Christmas compilation, aren't you?" she asked.

Walter leaned back in his wheelchair a bit, smiling softly. "Not quite yet. Haven't gotten into the living room so far."

"Well, Merry Christmas to you anyway, handsome."

Though he was in his kitchen, and Natalie some miles away, he blushed a bit regardless. She could always do that to him. Walter Slikowski did not have the kind of personality that invited flattery, or flirting. On those rare occasions when either came his way, he never quite knew how to deal with them.

"Thank you," he said at length. "I'm glad you called, actually. I spoke to a colleague yesterday, and she's going to help me take a closer look at the crime scene. I hope to do that tomorrow. If there's anything—"

"Walter."

He blinked, furrowed his brow. "Yes?"

"Are you doing anything at all today? Anything Christmasy?"

For a moment he wasn't sure how to respond. "Not precisely," he said at length. "Though I had planned to spoil myself with a full holiday meal on the guest plates. Perhaps a cocktail afterward. Oh, and the music, of course."

He was only half joking. Well, not joking at all, really, but putting a bit of humor in his voice so she wouldn't realize the part about using the guest plates was true. Nobody else was around, but it was still Christmas, after all. He'd stayed home, but it would be nice to at least feel a little festive. Walter was about halfway through this thought process when Natalie cut in.

"Would you like some company?"

"I—I'm sorry, what?" he asked sincerely, for he wasn't quite sure he'd heard her correctly.

"Well, I don't want to intrude, but I'm not doing a damned thing today. My brother died, so everyone I know thinks they can't invite me to do anything where I'm supposed to be happy, and what little family I have left agrees. I just thought—"

"Of course," Walter replied abruptly. "I'd love to have you join me. I won't have to eat leftover turkey all next week."

"Oh, well, glad I can be of assistance," Natalie said sarcastically.

He flushed. "You know I didn't mean that to be the only reason I want you to come."

There was a brief silence on the other end. "I know," Natalie said.

Her voice held an odd mix of sadness and humor.

"Why don't you come by around two o'clock?" he suggested.

"I'll be there with bells on," she replied.

It being Christmas, and knowing Natalie, he wasn't certain whether or not he should take the statement literally. He needn't have worried, however. When she finally arrived, the sounds of jazz and the scent of cooking turkey filling the apartment, Natalie was dressed as elegantly as ever. She looked beautiful.

Walter had to remind himself several times that she was there as a friend, seeking solace, and nothing more. That was how she had come to his door, and that was how she would leave.

He couldn't decide how to feel about that.

One thing was for certain, however. It made for a very interesting Christmas.

When Jenna and her mother came home from Uncle Brian's, they were both walking considerably slower than when they had left. Jenna had the top button on her black pants undone, the green sweater she wore covering up nicely. She'd had three servings of turkey, with salty, thick gravy, and two large servings of mashed potatoes, not to mention stuffing, green beans, squash, and carrots.

That was before dessert.

"Oooh," she moaned as she slumped on the living room couch. "I don't think I'll ever look at strawberry shortcake and not feel completely disgusted."

April laughed. Her personal downfall had been the pecan pie à la mode, but Jenna could see that her mom was feeling just about as gross as she was.

"It really is revolting, isn't it? Gorging like that?" April asked.

"It's Christmas," Jenna replied. "There's some kind of rule that says you're supposed to eat until you feel like throwing up."

April laughed, but only for a second. She grew a bit pale and held a hand across her stomach. "I'm thinking about going down and getting on the treadmill for about three days."

Jenna grinned. "Yeah? I'd like to see that."

"I said I was thinking about it," her mother replied. "I didn't say I was crazy enough to do it."

They lazed about for a short while. Eventually, Jenna stirred. If she didn't, she was afraid she might fall asleep early and be up in the middle of the night.

"I guess I should call Damon," she announced, though she hoped to find a message from him.

"Tell him I said hello," her mother said. "Of course, you've yet to introduce me to him. Your father's met him, but Mom? Oh, she's not important."

Jenna shot her a hard look and headed for the kitchen. The wall phone was also the answering machine. The light was blinking, which was a relief. There were five messages. Two were from colleagues of April's, the third was from her father. He'd called to wish them both a merry Christmas and to find out if Jenna liked her present. She smiled just hearing his voice.

The fourth was Damon.

"Hey, Jenna. I'm sorry I missed you. I'm going to my grandparents' house, and I don't think we'll be back until really late. If it's before, say, ten, I'll give you another try. Otherwise, call me in the morning. Our plane leaves in the late afternoon, and I want to give you a number you can reach me at in Captiva.

"I miss you."

Jenna smiled, though she was disappointed that she probably wouldn't get to speak with him until the morning.

The fifth message was from Moira.

"Jenna, are you there? If you're there, you have *got* to pick up."

Moira sounded as though she had been crying.

"Jenna, pick up . . . oh, man. All right, look, when you get home, call me. It doesn't matter what time, okay? Just call me as soon as you get in."

Her mother came into the kitchen behind her. "Wow. I hope everything's all right. What do you think that's about?"

Frowning, Jenna stared at the phone. When she went to pick it up, she had a sick feeling in the pit of her stomach that had nothing to do with Christmas dinner.

chapter 5

By the time Natalie left Walter's apartment, it had long since grown dark outside. They had shared a very pleasant Christmas meal together in the early afternoon, accompanied by a bottle of Piesporter Michelsberg, a sweet German wine that was a favorite of Walter's. Natalie offered to clear the dishes, and it was a testament to the relationship they'd once shared that he let her do it. Ever since he'd been confined to his wheelchair, he had been at pains not to let anyone do anything for him that he could possibly do for himself.

With Natalie, it was different. She had no pity for him. She offered out of simple courtesy and expediency. If she did the dishes, it would go faster.

While she cleaned up, Walter changed the musical selection. The Christmas jazz CDs had run their course, so he picked out an old Miles Davis set he liked. There were things he might have put on that would have been more romantic, but that wasn't why Natalie was there. He knew that. Still, the temptation was ever present.

Her brother had been murdered only a few days earlier. Even if there ever would be a chance for them—which Walter didn't believe—now was not it. So the music was chosen for aesthetics, not romance.

After Natalie cleaned up, they sat together in the living room. One window was open a crack to let in the crisp winter air, and the radiators in the old apartment were rattling overtime to keep up. The smell of the breeze, with a hint of fireplace smoke from nearby homes, combined with the warm, familiar smell of the radiators, and the music, and the wine, to make it perhaps the most pleasant conversation Walter had had in years.

It had been an almost perfect afternoon. They talked with the freedom of those who had once been intimate, and he was able to let his guard down in a way that had become quite rare for him. He comforted her as much as he could when she grieved for her brother, and he grieved with her as well. Natalie wanted to know all about his work and his life, if he'd ever fallen in love again, and how that had gone.

Walter assumed his answers had bored her horribly, but Natalie had managed to smile and nod through it all. Though they hadn't seen each other in so very long, he realized that she was a good friend to him still.

"It's so nice to have you here, to talk with you like this," he said at one point. "I wish we'd never lost touch. I feel like I missed out."

"You did," she promised, "but not on the whole friendship thing. I'm not sure we could have been very good friends if we'd kept in touch right after we parted ways. Too many hard feelings."

But those hard feelings were gone now, leaving only a sweet fondness that he found himself instantly treasuring.

In the early evening they broke out some of the leftovers from their earlier meal, and Walter made coffee. By the time Natalie bent to kiss his cheek, smiled tiredly, and confessed that she really did have to go home, it was after eight o'clock.

Natalie stood in the open door, elegant as always, and studied him a moment. Walter tried to read the expression on her face. There seemed to be a bit of sadness there, though a tiny smile played around the corners of her mouth. With a start, he realized that her expression was a mirror of his own, and she was feeling the same bittersweet emotions that filled him now that she was leaving.

It had been so nice, having her there, learning that a true and valuable friendship existed between them. But it was also a reminder that he lacked that sort of relationship with a woman he could fall in love with, and who might fall in love with him. His brother often urged him to get out, to meet people, to date, but somehow, it never seemed that simple.

"Natalie . . ."

She chuckled. "Don't get crazy on me, Walter," she told him. "I'll talk to you in a couple of days. Maybe we could go to a movie or something?"

He nodded. "I'd like that."

Then he sat and watched her move carefully down the walk. It had grown quite cold after dark, and the sheen of snow that remained after the landlord's meager effort at shoveling turned icy. When Natalie made it to her car, Walter breathed a sigh of relief.

As she drove away, he still had that bittersweet expression on his face.

In the Blakes' kitchen, Jenna and her mother stood in silence for a moment as the frantic tone of Moira's message sank in. It was just after eight-thirty. There was a queasy feeling in Jenna's stomach as she lifted the phone from its cradle and dialed seven digits she had known by heart for more than ten years.

As she listened to the ringing on the other end of the line, she turned and leaned against wallpaper with an ocean theme. It had been there forever, and Jenna didn't even notice it anymore.

April watched her with eyebrows raised. "No answer?"

"Must be on the other line or—"

"Hello?"

"Moira, it's me."

A tiny sound came over the phone from Moira, a little sigh of relief and frustration.

"Oh, God, Jenna, have you heard? Have you talked to anyone?"

"No. What's going on?" Jenna asked, feeling a little frantic herself now as Moira's obvious agitation began to infect her.

"Oh, God," Moira said again. There came another sigh, as she attempted to gain control of her emotions. When she spoke again, her voice was steady, but the frenzied Moira of a moment before lurked just beneath the surface.

"Last night, Chris Meserve . . . the police are saying he killed his family. All of them."

Horrified, Jenna gave a little gasp. Holding the phone tightly to her ear, she turned to stare at her mother. April was watching her with anxious curiosity.

"How do they . . . I mean, are they sure it was him?" Jenna asked.

"They had everybody coming over for Christmas today," Moira explained. "I guess . . . I heard his uncle found them. Chris was still in the house. He just . . ." Moira began to cry softly, her voice hitching. "He freaked out or something. Went postal. My mother heard he hasn't said a word to anyone, just sits there. I guess it'll be on the news tonight."

For a few seconds Jenna found she couldn't speak. She wanted to. Her mouth opened. There was even a tiny sound that came from her throat. But words would not come. Phone pressed to her ear, she stood leaning against that old ocean wallpaper, staring at her mother.

"What is it, honey?" April asked. "What happened?"

On the phone, she heard Moira say her name. Jenna blinked, shaken from the shock that had settled over her like a layer of ice.

"Oh, God, Moi," she whispered. Then she cleared

her throat, trying to sound more normal, trying to deal with the news. "That's unbelievable. I mean, we were just with him last night. He was at *your house*."

"Don't remind me," Moira replied, and it was more plea than sarcasm.

"So they're saying he's catatonic or something?"

"Or something. I don't know. I just . . . God, it's so creepy," Moira said.

Jenna could almost hear her friend shudder over the phone.

"Look, my mother's right here, wondering what the hell's going on. Let me go, and I'll give you a call in the morning," she said.

Moira was reluctant, but a few moments later Jenna hung up the phone and turned to face April. Together, almost as though they'd agreed to do so, they moved to the kitchen table and sat down.

"You remember Chris Meserve?" Jenna began.

Then she told her mother all of it. April was horrified. She stood up, pacing a bit, anxious to speak to other parents. If they'd all still been in high school, Jenna was sure her mother would be calling a parent-teacher meeting to discuss counseling for the students. But that kind of thing was all done with. They were adults now. When something horrible happened, they didn't have anyone to hold their hands and tell them it was going to be all right.

Except the most important people.

April glanced down at her daughter and saw that Jenna had tears in her eyes. Immediately, she sat down again. She reached out, and Jenna gratefully grabbed her mother's hands and bent over, crying silently. There was a pain in her stomach from clenching her muscles. Then she moved forward even farther. April slid her arms around Jenna, who fell into her mother's embrace as she had been doing ever since she could walk.

"Oh, Jenna," April whispered. "I'm sorry. It's so . . . hideous."

For a minute or two they just stayed like that. Jenna quickly got hold of herself and sat up to wipe the tears from her eyes. A kind of numbness enveloped her. Chris was—had been—a friend. She'd met his family, knew his little sister. The idea that he could have done something so horrible was beyond her capacity to imagine.

But that wasn't the worst of it.

"Mom?" she whispered. "It follows me, doesn't it?"

April stiffened, eyes widening as she stared at Jenna. "What are you talking about?"

Jenna swallowed hard. "It's like, ever since I started working with Slick . . . murder and insanity are just everywhere. With Melody, and . . . and now I come home . . . and it's here, too. It's like it's . . ."

She couldn't say anything more. Her throat closed up and tears streamed down her cheeks again. April seemed ready to comfort her again, but Jenna hugged herself tightly, sitting up straight.

"It isn't you, Jenna," her mother said, horrified. "How can you even think that? Of course it's not you. Things have been crazy. The world is . . . you've seen things nobody your age should ever have to see."

"But that's the job," Jenna said coldly, wiping away tears again. "That's my job. And that's the way I want it. But I've got to tell you, I never expected this."

After a long pause she met her mother's gaze directly.

"It's Christmas," Jenna said, and she couldn't keep the pain out of her voice.

There were very few cars out that night, even on the main roads. Those that did venture out into the world were occupied mainly by holiday revelers heading home from family gatherings. Minivan- and station wagon– and SUV-loads of families headed home after a long Christmas day, with children asleep in car seats or scrunched up against the safely locked doors, snoring softly, their favorite gifts from Santa piled around them.

The dark green Ford sedan that turned down Blackberry Lane had no children in it, however. No children, no presents, nor any holiday sentiment at all, only grumbling from the two men in the front seat about not being home where they belonged. When they came in sight of the split-level set back from the road at 42 Blackberry, however, the men fell silent. There was police tape across the front door of the house. A patrol car sat vigilantly in the driveway, the officer inside likely sipping coffee and reading the sports page by the dome light, which silhouetted him even now.

The sedan glided to a stop in front of the house, beside the small snowbank created by the plows in the early hours of that morning. Right about the time Chris Meserve was slaughtering his family.

Both doors opened simultaneously. Detective Mike Brody stepped out on the driver's side. He was a heavyset man in his late forties, and the burst veins in his nose gave him away as a closet drinker. Never on the job, though. His partner, Vic Grillo, stepped out of the passenger-side door. Grillo was almost the same age as Brody, but he looked a decade younger. His hair was still dark and full, and he kept in shape, working out in a makeshift gym in his basement. Both men wore suits, but Brody had a way of making even a brand-new suit look rumpled, while Grillo always looked more like a businessman than a cop.

That last might have had something to do with the fact that Grillo's marriage had survived his career as a suburban homicide detective, while Brody's had not. Actually, neither of Brody's marriages had survived. He was fond of saying that he was past marrying age. It would have been more accurate to say that he just didn't have the energy to care anymore. He had family, he had friends, and he had his job. It was all the life he hoped for, now that the distance to fifty could be counted in months.

Despite their differences, though, Brody and Grillo were friends. They'd been partners for nine years. That long, and it's either friendship or fistfights. In nine years, they'd seen a lot of death, a lot of murder. An ugly business, often a disgusting one.

As they stood on the lawn in front of the Meserves' house, Grillo wished he could pretend that what had happened there was the worst thing he'd ever seen. But he'd have been lying to himself if he thought that. There had been worse.

Three years earlier, a thirteen-year-old girl had shot her grandparents to death, then hung herself from an attic beam over on Oak Street. A couple of years before that, there'd been the little girl who'd been molested so badly that it killed her. Grillo had never wanted to beat anyone as badly as he'd wanted to beat her father. In the early nineties, not long after he and Brody had become partners, there'd been the rape and murder of a local girl and her boyfriend by a gang. The boyfriend was a member, and he'd been informing on them to the local authorities.

That had been the messiest crime scene Grillo had ever come across. He still dreamed about it sometimes. The last time had been more than a year ago, and it was the first time he had that dream that he hadn't woken up with tears in his eyes. It had worried him, actually, that he could have that dream, that nightmare, and not cry.

By comparison, the mess Chris Meserve had made of his family and his home was relatively simple. That didn't make it any easier to take, or to see, or to investigate. It had been a brutal, disgusting crime.

Vic Grillo knew he wasn't the best detective in the world, or even in eastern Massachusetts. Hell, probably even in Natick. And he sure as hell knew that that honor didn't go to Brody, either. But they did their job, and they tried their damndest.

"What the hell we doing here, Vic?" Brody grunted.

"We got the kid in lockup. You oughta be home with your family. We can pick this up in the morning."

Grillo nodded thoughtfully. "Going home. Absolutely. But you know as well as I do, Mike, that the first thing the lieutenant is going to ask us in the morning is why the Meserve kid lost his mind. Be nice if we had some kind of answer for him, wouldn't it?"

Brody only sighed. Together, they walked across the snow-covered lawn toward the house. The officer in the patrol car climbed out and started in their direction.

"Just us, Martin," Brody growled.

"Oh, hey, Detective. You guys need anything?"

"We'll let you know," Brody told him.

The detectives went up to the front door, reached over the police tape, and turned the knob. They ducked under the tape—Brody grunting with the effort of bending down—and went inside. Grillo flipped on the lights.

Upstairs, they went from bedroom to bedroom, where the mattresses were soaked with blood. In the living room, there were a great many unopened presents under the tree. Grillo figured they'd be donated to some charity, and hoped whoever got them wouldn't know where they'd come from. It was ghastly.

Though they had been through the Meserve kid's room earlier that day and brought a number of things back with them as potential evidence, the detectives had agreed that another walk-through was necessary. With the crime scene guys buzzing around, it was hard to really take it all in, to begin to react, beyond the obvious revulsion, to what had happened in that house.

Now they spent twenty minutes just lingering in the killer's room. The kid hadn't spoken since his arrest. They had no reason to think that he would speak soon, if ever again. But there would be a lot of people searching for explanations, not just the lieutenant. It would be helpful if the investigating detectives could offer those explanations.

Grillo hadn't a clue. From the look on his partner's face, he didn't think Brody had one either. There was nothing in Chris Meserve's room to indicate a pattern of violent behavior from the kid, or that the murders were a culmination of anything. Nothing to show that he was a disturbed individual, capable of such a thing. There were sports posters, trophies, clothes, videotapes, and compact discs.

No weapons. No fetish magazines. No black clothing except for one pair of ragged jeans at the bottom of a drawer. Not a damn thing.

Eventually they made their way into the basement rec room. There was a pool table there, along with an enormous entertainment center complete with widescreen TV, VCR, and all the latest video game apparatus.

Grillo rolled his eyes. He looked at Brody. "Video games. This is all we've got, isn't it? Christ, Mike, I don't want to be the one to suggest the kid was influenced by video games."

"Then don't," Brody snapped. "We have no proof of that, anyway."

"We've got nothing," Grillo agreed. "No diary, no notes, no self-mutilation. Just a nice, normal, athletic kid dealing with his first year in college, who just happens to massacre his family."

Brody went over to a large case that held two tall stacks of video game cartridges. He began to go through them as Grillo looked around the room some more, searching for any kind of inspiration. Grillo started wondering if it had been ridiculous to come out here. Brody was right, after all. He should be home with his family.

"Anything?" he asked.

"Mostly sports stuff. A few fantasy games. Like that," Brody replied. "We got nothing, Vic. Let's . . ." His words trailed off.

"What?" Grillo demanded, moving toward his partner.

"Let's see." Brody turned on the television, then popped the video game into the machine. He handed Grillo the box.

"Bloodlust?" Grillo read. "That sounds like a nice game."

Brody pressed Start on the unit, and the television came to life with the opening images of the game. A shadowy form—given the point of view, this was obviously meant to be the player—moved through a dark house with a long butcher knife. Into a bedroom. A scantily clad girl leaped up from her bed and ran screaming into the bathroom. The player—knife in hand—was meant to give chase.

Grillo turned to stare at Brody, open-mouthed.

"Who makes this crap?" he asked.

"Better question," Brody replied, "who plays it?"

With a shake of his head and a deep sigh, Grillo tossed the box on the floor. "Mike, no video game made this kid a killer. Come on. I hate the people who try to blame it all on the media and entertainment. We don't even know that he played the game."

Brody said nothing.

On the screen, the test run of the game showed a police officer coming through the door, only to be stabbed in the heart by the knife-wielding player.

Grillo flinched as he watched it.

"Come on," he said to his partner. "I want to go home."

Half a mile from the Meserves' house, the Gage family was still celebrating Christmas. It was nearly ten o'clock, but Cathy Gage—who was a single mom since her husband had bailed on her nine years earlier—and her two sons sat watching *The Santa Clause* on cable. About halfway through the movie, though, her elder son, John, got up, stretched, and went into his room, leaving Cathy and fourteen-year-old Danny to watch the rest of the movie alone.

In his room, John spent twenty minutes going through the stash of gifts he'd gotten that day. It had been a good Christmas. There were a lot of discs, new sneakers, several pairs of jeans, and a steel watch that he loved. It was just like the watch he remembered his father wearing, back when he was still around. There was a new basketball. There were clothes his mother had picked out, some of which had to go back and some of which were, surprisingly, not bad.

As he went through the few videos he'd received, he noticed the one that had caught his eye earlier. It was some kind of bootleg or something.

Curious, he slipped it into the VCR in his room.

In the morning he was the only member of the Gage family still alive.

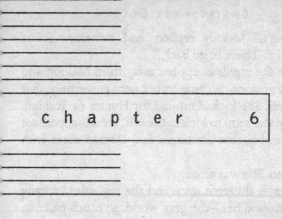

c h a p t e r   6

The morning after Christmas, Jenna dreamed about Melody LaChance. In the dream, the sun was out. It was warm and fine, the Fourth of July, though Jenna didn't know how she knew that. The girls were white-water rafting, just the two of them. There was joy in the dream, a surging bliss that is often found in dreams and so rarely in real life.

Then the dream changed.

Melody wasn't in the raft anymore. Jenna searched frantically, paddling, trying to keep herself upright in the raft. On the far bank of the river, she saw Melody standing, smiling and waving to her. Sadly, Jenna dropped her paddle and waved back.

"Come with me," Jenna whispered, though Melody was too far away to hear her even if she shouted.

It didn't matter. Melody heard. Impossibly, Jenna could see that she smiled.

"I can't," Melody replied, and somehow Jenna heard her. "I have to go back."

Then the rapids swept her away from Melody, and Jenna was alone. It came to her very powerfully, that aloneness. She looked around for Hunter or Yoshiko. Quickly, she spun to look in the raft, thinking, perhaps unreasonably, that she might find Damon there with her.

But no. She was alone.

Her eyes fluttered open and the real world sprang to life around her—the gray world, so much paler, in its way, than the vivid universe of her dreams. Jenna clutched the stuffed Pooh bear to her chest and looked around at the things she had left in her room. Not much. Some books. A puzzle version of an old Monet painting that she'd glued down and hung on the wall. Stuffed animals.

Real. All around her. Real, tangible things; parts of her life.

The sun shone through the windows, but it did not take away the feeling that the world around her was somehow tarnished, somehow less than what she had just left.

Melody, smiling. The Fourth of July. The river, which had smelled, strangely, like the ocean. The splash of water on her face.

Of course, Jenna had known Melody for only a few weeks, all told. September and October, and most certainly not July. In her dream, Jenna had been joyous and sorrowful, and upon waking, her emotions did not change.

Thoughts of Melody brought both feelings upon her.

Of course, it had only been a dream. Melody was dead. And Jenna had never been white-water rafting. Suddenly, however, she felt the urge to give it a try.

It'll have to wait until spring, she thought.

There was a light tap on her door. As Jenna yawned and began to roll over, her mother slowly pushed the door open.

"Honey, you up?" April asked.

Jenna stretched. When she replied, her voice had a sleepy groan in it. "Barely," she said. "What time is it?"

"Time to get up," her mother said, a wry grin on her face. "Your boyfriend's on the phone."

"Damon?" Jenna's eyebrows went up, a tiny, excited smile forming on her lips.

"You have another one?"

Jenna threw back the covers and shot up from the bed. Her hair was wild from sleep, and her faded teddy bear nightshirt—which had always been one of her favorites—had several small holes worn through the cotton. She hesitated a moment before shaking her head and feeling silly. It didn't matter how she looked. Damon was on the phone calling from Florida and couldn't exactly see her.

"You want to take it in my room?" April asked.

"No. I'm coming down anyway," Jenna told her mother. She went down the stairs and into the kitchen, her mother following her. "I didn't hear the phone ring."

"Call waiting. I was on the other line. He didn't want me to get you up, but it's nearly ten o'clock, so—"

"Ten!" Jenna cried. "I'm a total slug. God. I'm supposed to meet Slick at one o'clock, and—"

Jenna stopped herself mid-sentence. The sudden realization that she had slept so late and the anxiety created by what that was already going to do to her day were dispersed the instant Jenna's hand touched the phone. There were things she had to get to, but they could wait.

"He's very nice," April whispered.

With a grin, Jenna put the phone to her ear.

"Hey," she said. "Have you ever been white-water rafting?"

On the other end of the line, Damon chuckled softly. "What? What are you talking about?"

"White-water rafting," she repeated. "Have you ever been, and do you want to go with me?"

"During the winter?"

Jenna frowned. "When it's warm, goofball."

She heard Damon laugh again. It was a good sound, a warm and intimate sound that she had missed, even for the few days they'd been apart. With all that had been going on, first with Slick and Mayor Kerchak, then with Priya, and now Chris Meserve killing his family, Jenna's mind had been on anything but Damon.

Now, though . . .

"It's warm here," he said. "I'm going parasailing tomorrow. There were dolphins jumping just off the coast as we drove down from Fort Myers yesterday."

"Rub it in, why don't you?"

He laughed again, warm and gentle.

"God, it's good to hear your voice," she found herself saying, without even realizing the words were going to translate from her mind to her mouth.

Embarrassed, she glanced up but found that her mother had left the room. Jenna was relieved, but not completely. Damon hadn't responded immediately, and the lag in time was uncomfortable.

"So, rafting?" Damon said thoughtfully. "This summer. Planning kind of ahead, aren't we?"

A sick feeling spread through her stomach. *No. Don't do this,* she thought, angry at Damon. Why even ask that question, if he didn't feel like they were in a position where they *could* plan ahead?

"You have other plans?" she asked, with as much false bravado as she could muster.

"None," Damon assured her. "Just taking a moment to like the idea of you figuring to spend the summer hanging with me. Especially so far in advance."

Jenna breathed a sigh of relief. "Okay, maybe not the whole summer. I mean, me, Massachusetts, you, somewhere in Jersey. But plans are good."

"I agree completely."

The two of them fell quiet a moment, enjoying the tacit acknowledgment that their relationship was a serious one, that neither of them had any doubt of its immediate future. After a moment, though, Damon broke the silence, his voice having taken on a much graver tone.

"So, what's going on there, Jenna? What happened with this kid, Meserve?"

Jenna blinked in surprise. "It's on the news there, already?"

"Everything ugly is on the news. They don't care where it happens. They want to bring us tragedy and human suffering twenty-four/seven. I think that's going to be its own cable channel soon."

"Did we wake up on the cynical side of bed this morning?" Jenna asked, taken aback slightly by the bitterness in Damon's tone.

"Just wishing you could have had a normal Christmas, that's all."

With a sigh and a nod he wouldn't be able to see, Jenna told Damon all about Chris Meserve. She told him about Priya and Mayor Kerchak and that she missed him terribly. Then she confessed that she thought the ugliness of her job had followed her home.

"Come on," Damon argued. "Your being around didn't have anything to do with that kid going crazy."

Jenna knew he was right. It was just that she had been filled with such pleasant anticipation about Christmas. She had thought that it would be a return, in some way, to the wonder and innocence and happiness of the years she'd spent growing up in her mother's house. And in some ways it had been.

But she wasn't a little girl anymore. Her mother couldn't protect her from everything anymore.

"I guess I just wish there was a Santa Claus," she said tiredly. "So shoot me."

They chatted for a while longer, about what they'd

gotten for Christmas and when Damon would be back on campus. Classes resumed in two weeks, but dorms reopened several days earlier. Jenna planned to go back the first day she'd be able.

"I promised my mom we'd have dinner with her as soon as you're back," she told him.

"I look forward to it," Damon replied. "She seems nice."

"Of course. She's my mom."

The doorbell rang then, and she promised to call Damon the following day; then she hung up quickly. When she went into the living room, she saw her mother holding the door open in an obvious state of distress. Moira stood in the open door, her arms wrapped around her belly.

"Moi?" Jenna ventured. "What happened?"

Somehow, she knew what the answer was going to be.

"It happened again," Moira said, wiping away tears. "John Gage killed his family last night."

No matter how many people sang "White Christmas" each year, it was not all that common for the Boston area to be blanketed with snow when December 25 rolled around. It happened, certainly, but odds were better for a brown Christmas.

Walter had enjoyed the snow, but he knew it couldn't last. In comparison to some of the storms he'd seen roll through New England since he'd lived there, the previous day's snowfall had been a dusting. Now, as he sat in his chair and looked out the window, he knew it was all going away. The sky was clear, the sun heating the pavement and the ground, even through the snow. Across the street, he could see wet black shingles on roofs, melting snow running into gutters. Grass poked up through the crusty covering at odd intervals, in queerly patterned stretches that were growing even as he watched.

Walter smiled. The snow had arrived for the holiday, and now it was going away as quickly as it had come. Almost as if it had been a gift, a reward to those who had hoped and prayed for white. A present for romantics.

Romantics.

With a scowl, he shook his head. He was thinking about Natalie again and realized that he was being a fool. There could be nothing new between them, except perhaps real friendship. That would be enough for him, though. It would have to be. The past was filled with misgivings, and neither of them would want to start down that path again.

Nodding silently to himself, Walter pushed himself back, and then turned to propel himself down the hallway toward his bedroom. He would want lunch soon, and shortly thereafter, Jenna would arrive. While he waited, he thought he might try to get some reading done.

With the exception of Natalie's visits, he'd thought of little over the past few days besides the murder of Jim Kerchak. Nor had the city of Somerset for that matter. Jim's upcoming funeral was turning out to be a Boston media spectacle, and the swearing in of the former deputy mayor into the city's top spot the previous day had been only a part of it. But Walter's grief had been more private. The city had known Jim Kerchak as its mayor, but he had known the man as a friend.

Of course, the fact that Natalie was his sister meant that even the pleasure of having her around was informed by the specter of Jim's death and the lack of any substantial theory as to the identity of his murderer.

It was rare that Walter allowed himself to be reminded of his handicap, even more so that he allowed such a reminder to make him feel helpless in any way. When he realized that he could not effectively investigate Kerchak's murder because he did not have the use of his legs, the fact had disturbed him greatly.

As usual, however, Jenna had seen things from another angle. Just because he couldn't see the crime scene with his own eyes didn't mean he couldn't see it through someone else's—or, more accurately, through the lens of a video camera. He had gone over the police report again and again, but it had yielded no real clue as to who had killed the mayor, or why.

All he could do now was wait for Jenna to arrive. The time would pass more quickly if he had a book in his hand.

Before he could reach his room, however, the phone rang. Walter turned his chair toward the kitchen. There were several old friends he had neglected to call on Christmas Day, mainly because of Natalie's presence, and he expected it would be one of them. An even better way to pass the time—catching up with old friends.

"Hello."

"Dr. Slikowski, it's Jenna."

Walter frowned. "Is everything all right? I would have thought you'd be en route by now."

Her reply was preceded by a short, hitching breath, almost a gasp, and he realized that she had been crying.

"It's . . . I've had a pretty tough couple of days. I was wondering if you'd mind . . . if we could do it a little later."

An anxious feeling of protectiveness stole over Walter immediately. Jenna was more than an employee, she was a sort of protégée, and her welfare was of great concern to him. Walter knew that she had plenty of people to look out for her. He also knew that there were a great many she would open up to before she would reveal her concerns to him. Even so, he wanted to soothe her.

"Of course," he said immediately. "Or not at all. I could postpone it until tomorrow, if that would be better."

Even as he said those words, Walter regretted them. He had been willing to wait through Christmas day, knowing the weather and the loss of time might cost him any chance of finding a clue that would help the investigation. Another day could only make it worse.

But whatever was bothering her, Jenna was not so distracted that she didn't realize that.

"No, no. You can't afford another day. And the mayor's funeral is tomorrow anyway. I'll be there. Just . . . could you give me until three o'clock? We should still be able to get over to City Hall and have a look around before it gets too dark."

"Of course," Walter agreed. "I'll just have to call Detective Gaines."

"Audrey? What for?"

"Well, aside from the equipment she's lending us, having a detective with us will prevent any questions about what we're doing poking around at the scene of the crime."

After a pause, Jenna cleared her throat. "I'll be there," she said weakly.

"Jenna, you still haven't told me what's going on. Are you all right? Can I help in any way?"

Her laugh was halfhearted, pained. "I know you don't really watch much television, and Mayor Kerchak's murder has been the top story the last couple of days, but I'm surprised you haven't read about it in the paper."

Walter could only listen, then, as Jenna related the horrors that had been unfolding in her town over the previous days. Two of her former classmates had gone on murderous rampages in as many days, killing their respective families.

Though he was awkward with such things, he did try to comfort her. He realized that he had been even more wrapped up in the aftermath of Jim Kerchak's death than he'd known—or paying less attention to the news because of it. In the end, however, his mind returned to the details, to the circumstances of the murders Jenna had described.

"It certainly doesn't sound like a coincidence," Walter said gently.

"No, it doesn't," Jenna agreed. "I'm going to try to get some more details, maybe talk to people I know, find out if they've been hanging around together, acting weird or anything."

Walter frowned. "Maybe you should let the police handle it," he suggested.

Jenna grew angry. "Like you're letting them handle Mayor Kerchak's murder?" she demanded.

"That's different," he replied, though his defense sounded weak even to his own ears. "I've been asked to consult in this case. Natick isn't even within my jurisdiction, so it isn't as though you could tell the police we were working on it together."

"These were my friends, Dr. Slikowski," Jenna said coldly. "I've known both of them almost my entire life. I know everybody says that. "Oh, he was such a nice boy, a quiet neighbor, a polite kid,' whatever. Maybe that's the case. Maybe they both just lost it. But I think something's going on here, and I can't sit on my hands. I have to take a closer look."

Walter massaged the bridge of his nose. His wire-rim glasses were on the bureau in his room, and now he wondered if he hadn't had them off too long, for he was beginning to get a serious headache.

"Of course," he said tiredly. "Let me know if there's

anything I can do. We can talk about the case later if you like."

"Thanks," Jenna said softly. "I'll see you in a bit."

After Jenna hung up the phone, she went back out into the living room. Her mother and Moira were sitting on the sofa, cradling steaming cups of coffee. With her sad eyes wide with shock, Moira blew across the rim and carefully sipped from her mug. Jenna saw that her mother also wore that haunted expression, but instead of the empty, distant look in Moira's eyes, April's gaze was focused. She watched Moira with a mixture of sympathy and profound concern.

Jenna didn't blame her. Moira was not doing well with this. Not at all.

Who can blame her? I'm not exactly doing well myself.

Melody's murder was the worst thing that had ever happened to Jenna, no question about that. The fact that she had discovered that her friend was dead by walking in on her autopsy in progress only made it more horrible. But all of this was a close second. The two guys—the two killers—were boys she had known for years. Neither of them had been very close to her, but it was still inconceivable to think that they were capable of such atrocities.

How much worse, though, for Moira, who had never in her life known anyone who had been murdered.

Jenna sat down in the chair that was kitty-corner to the couch and put a hand on Moira's knee.

"Hey. It'll be all right," she said.

Moira stared at her dubiously, almost smirking. "Oh, sure. This'll all go away."

"That's not what I meant," Jenna replied calmly. "I'm . . . I'm freaked, too, Moi. But we'll be all right. I don't know how all this happened, how those guys could just snap like that, but—"

"This doesn't happen, J," Moira said suddenly. She glanced at April, then back to Jenna. "Grandparents die. Great-aunts. Sometimes, I guess, a kid you know from school or the neighborhood, like when Timmy McConville passed away in the seventh grade. Remember, he had that heart defect? I rode the bus with him every day. I know people die, Jenna.

"But not like this."

Jenna grimaced, took a deep breath, and sat back in her chair. "People die like this every day, Moi. Just not people we know."

Moira fixed her with a withering glare. "I guess this is easy for you, huh? You deal with murders and stuff all the time, right? It must be no big deal. Well, it's a big deal to me."

Jenna looked away as tears began to slide down her cheeks. She was sick at the thought of what Chris and John had done, to know that people she had spoken to, smiled at, kissed during spin-the-bottle and truth-or-dare games, could be capable of such horror.

Finally she turned back to Moira.

"You know better than that."

Moira began to sob. April had to grab the coffee mug from her hand to keep it from spilling all over the carpet. Then she got up and left the room as the two girls came together in an embrace, crying and whispering to each other.

After a while—Jenna would not have been able to say how long—they calmed themselves. Though their embrace ended, their hands were still entwined as they sat on the edges of their seats.

"How could they do it, Jenna? They're not killers. You know those two. They're just not," Moira said, her tone pleading for agreement.

Jenna gave it to her. "You're right. I don't know what's going on here, but I have a hard time believing those two guys just snapped. An even harder time believing they did it on purpose. It could be drugs, I guess. John sure wasn't any stranger to experimenting with whatever came along. But to drive them to this . . . I don't know.

"I plan to find out, though."

"Come on," Moira snorted. "What are you gonna do? I mean, I know you help out with autopsies and stuff at your job, but . . . I mean, you're eighteen, Jenna. You think the police are going to deputize you or something, 'cause you're a lab assistant?"

Jenna didn't even respond. She worked with Slick on more than autopsy results. When he was called in to consult on investigations, she helped, sometimes even when she wasn't asked. Moira knew that, but obviously she couldn't wrap her head around it. Jenna wasn't about to argue.

"It's a bit out of your league, isn't it?" Moira persisted.

"Yeah, I guess," Jenna replied. "I just figure it can't

hurt to look into it. Somebody has to find out why all this happened."

There must have been something in her voice, some doubt, for Moira, frightened, raised her head and gazed at Jenna, studying her eyes.

"You aren't convinced, are you?" she asked. "You think maybe Chris and John just did this, just killed their families in cold blood."

In her mind, Jenna heard Slick's voice, telling her never to come to any conclusion before the autopsy results were in, before the investigation was complete. She knew Moira needed reassurance, but she couldn't give it.

"I wish I knew."

chapter 7

Walter gritted his teeth and tried not to feel the eyes that gazed at him from the hallway. People walked past the open door of the audiovisual resource room in City Hall and tried their best not to stare in at him. But their best wasn't good enough. Some even stopped to stare for a few seconds. Detective Gaines had to close the door to get across the message that they were being rude.

Much as he hated to admit it, even to himself, Walter felt crippled. He sat in his wheelchair and watched as a tech rigged a TV and VCR to broadcast live from the video camera that sat on the table. When the tech was finished, he left the door open on his way out of the room.

Jenna picked up the video camera and hefted it as though testing its weight. Walter smiled at her, but he knew it would look forced. It was too bad. He'd missed having her around in the past few days. It was good to see her, even if only briefly, and even though she had problems of her own. Still, he had asked for her help, and she had come in spite of her troubles.

It meant a lot to him. Which was part of the reason he tried his best with a smile. The other part was that he didn't want anyone to notice his discomfort, not even Jenna.

But she saw it, in that smile. No doubt about it. Her response was not to smile in return, but to frown. She glanced at the open door, then back at him. A woman in an ill-fitting gray suit watched them curiously through the open door. This time, it was Jenna who closed it.

"So, we're all set then?" she asked, turning to Audrey.

When Walter smiled at Jenna again, there was a great deal more honesty in it.

"Almost," Audrey replied.

The detective picked up a headset from the table. She slipped it on and tapped at the earpiece lightly, then slid the small microphone into place in front of her mouth.

"Put these on," she said, handing one each to Jenna and Walter. "I borrowed these from the squad."

"Lieutenant Gonci didn't mind?" Walter asked, concerned.

"He doesn't know," Audrey replied. "But I don't think he would have minded if I'd bothered to ask him."

He took a deep breath as he slipped the headset on. "Audrey, thank you so much for helping today. It's probably nothing, and I want to tell you again that it has nothing to do with not trusting your work—"

"You don't have to apologize, Walter," Audrey said quickly. "I wanted you on that roof. Too bad when they retrofitted this building for wheelchair access, it never occurred to anyone that someone in a chair might need to get up there."

"A reasonable presumption," he admitted.

Still, it bothered him. The alternative was having someone carry him up the last few steps to the rooftop, and he wasn't about to do that. So this was it. Jenna's suggestion had been the only feasible one.

Audrey motioned for Jenna to follow her. "Let's get on with it, then."

With the video camera in her hands, and the headset on, Jenna felt more than a little silly. But in a way, she also thought it was kind of cool.

"I sort of feel like singing the *Mission: Impossible* theme," she said quietly.

Beside her, Audrey allowed a small grin.

"Singing it?" Slick said, his voice coming in loud and clear over the headset. "I didn't know it had any words."

"Humming it, then, Mr. Literal," Jenna retorted.

On the fourth floor, Audrey led her to the stairwell that would take them to the roof.

"Why don't you turn the camera on now, Jenna," she said. "Walter, let me know if you don't have a picture."

Jenna hit the Record button, and Slick confirmed that he did, indeed, have visual.

"Gotta love technology," Jenna whispered.

Audrey pointed to the bottom of the stairs, indicating that Jenna should focus there.

"The custodian arrives in the very early hours of the morning to clean up before anyone else can possibly get here," Audrey explained. "He was walking past the bottom of the stairs here when he felt a draft. As soon as he started up the stairs, he could see that the door was open, and—"

"At four o'clock in the morning?" Jenna asked.

She moved the camera so that she could see Audrey's thoughtful face through the lens, and so that Slick could see her as well.

"There are plenty of streetlights and parking lot light poles out in the square, plus the moon, I suppose," Audrey said. "Shall we go up?"

"Please," Slick replied over the headset connection.

Jenna led the way with the camera, sweeping it from side to side, hoping to give Slick as much visual information as she could. At the top of the stairs, she stopped so that Audrey could get by her and unlock the door.

"You said the lock wasn't broken," Slick said. "You're assuming some kind of internal involvement, then?"

Audrey opened the door, and it swung out over the roof. "Yes," she confirmed. "But not the custodian. We have a firm alibi for his whereabouts at the estimated time of death."

"Which was?" Jenna asked, sweeping the camera around the roof.

"Sometime between nine and eleven P.M.," Slick replied.

Jenna took that in as she looked around. It was cold on the roof, and getting late. It must have been nearly three-thirty, so they wouldn't have much time up there before it started to get too dark for the video camera to be of much use.

"Over here, Jenna," Audrey said.

She gestured to an area of the roof not far from the edge. Jenna walked toward her, feeling with her feet so she wouldn't trip over anything. There was a lot of stuff on the roof, including old desks and rusted filing cabinets, things she knew weren't supposed to be up there.

"This is the place," Audrey said.

"Jenna," Slick began, "give me a good view of the ledge, right up close, then pull back and get as much of the roof area around it as you can."

She did as he asked, moving as close to the edge as she dared. Through the viewer, she could see a long portion of the knee-high wall that ran around the roof. Certain areas of it were still damp.

"I don't know what we're thinking, coming up here," Jenna said. "I must have been nuts to suggest it. It's snowed, and now it's melted. We're not going to find anything."

"Be patient," Slick's voice said kindly in her ear.

"But not too patient," Audrey reminded. "We don't have a lot of time."

Jenna pulled the camera back, moving it around, showing as much as she was able of the area around the spot where the mayor's corpse had been thrown from the roof. But her mind wasn't completely on the job. There were so many other things warring for her attention. Chris Meserve and John Gage were primary among them, not to mention Priya's problems and her own wishes that classes would get under way again sooner rather than later, given how awkward things had been with her high school friends.

And something else, something nagging at the back of her mind. She couldn't quite put a finger on it, but something about the time of death bothered her. She and Slick had determined that the mayor did not die from the fall. His neck was broken, and his corpse left alone for hours before someone threw him off the roof. But—

"Y'know, I know it's government work—and no offense to the police, Audrey," she began, "but let's take the earliest possible T.O.D. here. Nine o'clock. Isn't it likely that some people were still working at that time of night?"

"Hmm," she heard Slick mumble. Then, "Audrey?"

Audrey was wandering around the roof. Jenna thought that she was searching for clues. A lot of cops, knowing that the crime scene had been gone over several times, wouldn't have bothered to do more than sit while the M.E. and his assistant got their jollies playing detective. But Audrey Gaines was a good cop. She was there, so she was looking around for something they might have missed before.

When the question arose, she barely acknowledged it. "We've been through the logs, questioned supervisors, all of that. Everything we can determine indicates that with the exception of the mayor and the director of development—who were in a meeting until shortly before nine—all employees had left the building by eight-fifteen."

"And the director of development—"

"Maureen Marchese," Audrey supplied. "We questioned her several times. Plus she has witnesses as to her whereabouts by nine-thirty. Technically, she's a suspect because she was the last person to see the mayor alive, she had a key to the building, all that. But trust me, she's no killer. Never mind that she isn't strong enough to have thrown the mayor off the building."

"I do trust you," Slick replied. "I just wish there were a simple answer to all this. I hope I didn't waste your time. Or yours, Jenna."

Jenna sighed and kept sweeping with the camera. It was several minutes before the silence was broken by a grunt from Slick. She knew that grunt. It was the M.E.'s version of "Eureka."

"Dr. Slikowski?" she asked.

"Jenna, do me a favor. Move to the center of the roof, please."

She did as he asked.

"Now lift the camera and give me a three-hundred-and-sixty-degree view of your surroundings."

Again she complied. It was starting to get dark, but she could still see very well through the camera. Mostly what she could see from up there were distant parts of the city. But to the north there was an apartment complex, and to the west there was an office building. Both were several stories higher than City Hall. There were even some blinds open in the apartment building, and it made her feel like a peeper.

"Walter, what's on your mind?" Audrey asked.

But Jenna thought she knew. She had the advantage of being able to see what Slick was seeing, at the same angle and everything. Focused. Whereas Audrey was used to seeing what was up there.

"One last question," Slick told her. "Where was the meeting between Miss Marchese and the mayor?"

"In the mayor's office," Audrey replied. "What's that got to do—"

"According to her," Slick said bluntly.

"Yeah. But we searched her office, too."

"For what?"

Audrey shook her head. "For any kind of documents that would prove she left later than she said, or had a grudge against the mayor or something. Where are you going with this?"

Jenna narrowed her eyes. "But you didn't search her office for signs of a struggle or anything?" she asked.

With a frown, Audrey shook her head. "You think she killed him? I'm telling you, that's just not the case. Now would you explain?"

Once again, Jenna turned the camera toward Audrey's face, so Slick could see her while he spoke.

"The killer or killers murdered the mayor, as we said, hours before he was thrown from the roof. And left him in one spot. Given all the debris that's up here and, more importantly, the fact that they would have had to realize that they stood a great risk of being seen from either the apartment building or the offices across the street, I think it's likely that they killed him inside the building. Then, hours later, when it would be far less likely that they would be seen, they threw him off the roof to imply suicide."

"Why bother, though?" Jenna asked, sweeping the camera around again. "If they thought that far ahead, they had to know a little bit about what they were doing. There had to be easier ways to try to fake his suicide if that's what they really wanted."

"Good question," Audrey admitted. "And if the mayor was killed inside the building, it's quite possible that it happened in Maureen Marchese's office."

"Even if she didn't kill him," Slick said, "it doesn't mean she doesn't know who did."

When Jenna arrived at Moira's that night, Noah and Priya were both there already. It was after eight, and the three of them were sitting around the Kearneys' basement listening to Blessid Union of Souls and playing darts. The smiles they managed when Jenna walked in were obviously rare for the evening.

"Hey," she said. "The wake continues, huh?"

Noah frowned. "Whoa. That's pretty cold, Jenna."

"No kidding," Moira said. "Sorry we can't all be so upbeat. Having people we know and trust turn into mass murderers kind of tarnishes the festivity of the season, y'know?"

Jenna held up a hand. "Cut it out, you guys. I know you're trashed by this whole thing. So am I. I just . . . I think there are better ways we can be there for each other than by feeding off each other's grief."

"Feeding off . . . what the hell does that mean?" Moira asked, studying Jenna as though she were a stranger.

"No, guys, wait," Priya said, speaking up. She had darts in her hands, but she wasn't focused on the board. She wasn't paying attention to anything but the carpeted floor just then. "Jenna's right."

"How's that, exactly?" Noah asked.

Finally Priya raised her head. There was a sad smile on her face. "We should do something. Not just sit around here. What those guys did, there's nothing we can do about it. It sucks, yeah. Talk about warping reality. But we can't let it take over our lives. We don't have much time together before you all have to go back to school. I know I'd like to do something with that time, even if it's just going to the movies. I'm not up for a party. I'm sure none of you is, either. But I wouldn't mind going out and getting a pizza. I'm starved."

Moira and Noah both nodded slowly. Jenna smiled at Priya, happy that she was there. And happy that she appeared to have come back into herself, in some way. On Christmas Eve, Jenna thought Priya had seemed like half a person. Now, despite her grief, she was Priya again.

"I'm kind of hungry myself," Jenna said. "Plus, I really need to talk to you guys about something."

Jenna drove them all in her father's car to Gaetano's Pizza, an old hangout from their high school days. It was a grease pit, but it had a nostalgic healing quality they all needed. While they waited, they carefully avoided the subject of the horrors from the past few days. But after the pizza was ready, and they started to dig in, Noah asked Jenna what she had wanted to talk to them about.

At first she glanced away.

"Jenna?" Priya asked. "What's wrong?"

"I just don't want to get us back on this subject, now that we seem to be cruising along nicely," she confessed.

"It's okay," Moira said, after they were all silent for a moment. "What, have you heard something?"

Jenna shook her head. "Not exactly. It's just . . ." One more deep breath, and then she gave voice to her thoughts. "Doing the job I do, seeing the stuff I see, I always figure that anything nasty happens and you've got to look at it twice, and then look at it again. A lot of times, things aren't what they seem. Especially if they seem suspicious right off the bat. Then, no matter how many people try to make sense of it for you, you've got to try to figure out what made it suspicious in the first place."

"What, you think Chris and John were in some kind of conspiracy?" Moira asked, sounding both doubtful and a little bit angry.

"No," Jenna said firmly. "I don't think that. We all know those two. We've all heard that they don't even seem to remember anything, that they're like catatonic or something. Okay, look. They're good, normal teenagers. No history of violence, no torturing small animals, no building weapons in their cellars. We know these guys. Do any of you think either of them is capable of something like this?"

Moira and Priya shook their heads. Noah hesitated. "Noah?"

"No," he confirmed. "But I don't think any of us knew them that well. I mean, have you ever met anyone you thought was probably a killer?"

"I have," Jenna replied. She paused to let that sink in, and then went on. "I've seen perfectly normal people do things that were horrible, vicious. People who would never have done anything like that if they were in their right minds. I met a woman who was dying and thought she could force her soul into someone else's body. I fought for my life against a guy who wanted to rip out my heart and eat it."

"Oh, my God," Priya whispered.

"If it were just Chris, or just John, it'd be easy to say, 'Wow, I guess we never really knew him.' But both of them, in the exact same scenario? I think it's too suspicious," Jenna went on. "I don't think either one of them was in his right mind when he did these things. And the coincidence is just too much. The cases are too similar. Which makes me wonder if there isn't a cause the police haven't considered, if they were exposed to something that made them so violent. Not something that influenced their actions, but actually caused them, literally changed their behavior.

"And if that's true, then I have to wonder if it was an accident, or something that was done to them on purpose."

Jenna took a breath, then glanced around at her

friends as her words sank in. A couple of times Noah looked as if he was going to say something, but each time his expression turned thoughtful again, and he remained silent.

Finally Priya spoke up.

"Don't you think the cops are checking into that possibility?" she asked.

"Maybe," Jenna said. "Maybe not. Some cops think around corners, but a lot of them get into patterns of thinking, based upon their expectations, which are based upon their experiences. Homicide cops, without a doubt, have seen a lot of people do barbaric, inhuman things. Why should they question it?"

"But you do?" Noah asked.

"Don't you?" Jenna replied. "Think about it."

Moira rubbed her eyes and stared at Jenna tiredly. "We are thinking about it, Jenna. I have to tell you, though, I, for one, think you're getting way too carried away with this job of yours. This is not where you work. This is your hometown. You're not a cop, you're somebody's lab assistant. What makes you think the cops can't solve a bunch of murders—murders there isn't really any mystery about to begin with—and *you* can?"

Jenna blinked, surprised by the sarcasm in Moira's voice.

"I . . . I just think, y'know, that they don't know Chris and John. But we *do* know better."

"So talk to the cops," Noah said. "I mean, what else are we supposed to do? We're not exactly the local crime watch, y'know?"

With a sigh, Jenna nodded. She picked up a piece of Hawaiian pizza and took a bite. For a long moment her friends waited, expecting her to go on, but she remained silent.

Suddenly she became painfully aware of how much she missed Hunter and Yoshiko.

The next morning Jenna woke up determined. She refused to allow her friends' doubts, and their insistence upon seeing her as nothing more than their eccentric friend from high school, to get in her way. Maybe the police would stop short of making assumptions that would handicap their case, and maybe they wouldn't.

If they never saw beneath the surface of what had happened to the Meserve and Gage families, Jenna was going to make certain it wasn't because she hadn't worked hard to bring it to their attention.

After April had left for the hospital, Jenna took a quick shower and put on just a dash of makeup. She put on a pair of stretch twill pants and a navy-blue turtleneck, then belted her black leather jacket over it. Before leaving, she looked at herself in the full-length mirror on the back of her mother's bathroom door.

"At least I don't look like I'm still in high school," she said aloud.

It had turned cold again overnight, and she had the heater up full blast. Icicles dangled from the fronts of houses and mailboxes and even from trees in some places, but the roads were clear.

Fortunately, she had never had reason to go inside

the police station while growing up in Natick. She had passed it hundreds of times as she took the bus to Natick High. Now, as she parked in the lot, across from a row of imposing patrol cars, she felt a nervous flutter in her chest.

Quit it, she told herself. *You're used to this. You've been dragged over the coals by the Cambridge cops, and inside plenty of police stations.*

All of which was true.

But, somehow, this was different. She wasn't the medical examiner's assistant out here. These cops didn't work with Slick; it wasn't even the same county. They would have no idea who he was, and no vested interest in listening to anything that Jenna had to say.

None at all. Here in Natick, she was just Jenna Blake, whose mother was a surgeon at the local hospital, and who had pretty much kept out of trouble in high school.

High school, which had not been very long ago at all.

Despite the fact that just the day before she had helped Slick in an investigation, with the complete cooperation of the detective involved, Jenna was anxious. As she stepped inside the station and glanced around for a duty officer to tell her how to find the detectives working the case, Jenna was tempted, for a moment, to turn and run out. To get in the car and drive home.

What stopped her wasn't her friendship with Chris or John. They hadn't really been that close. Nor was it any sense of duty, now that she had worked with Slick for so long. What stopped her from turning around was a combination of two things: the fact that there was a mystery here and it called out to her and—maybe even more important—the memory of the doubtful looks on her friends' faces when she tried to talk to them about it.

As if the very idea that she might be able to help were absurd.

We'll see, she thought as she spotted the desk sergeant and started toward him. *We'll just see.*

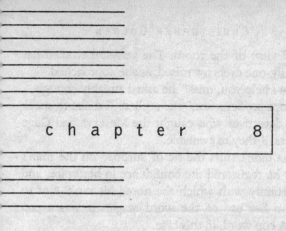

In a way Jenna was surprised not to see any reporters in the station. There was no doubt in her mind that this was the hottest story around at the moment. But instead of the chaos she expected from having visited the Somerset and Cambridge police stations, there was a kind of ho-hum routineness about the atmosphere inside the building. Still, she suspected it was only temporary—that the media were waiting to jump at any break in the case. They were probably standing on the front lawns of the friends and neighbors of the slain families.

Then she remembered that this morning was Mayor Kerchak's funeral, and all the Boston area news teams would be in Somerset for that.

Jenna slid past a couple of uniformed officers speaking in a heated whisper about something and went directly up to the sergeant, who sat behind a large desk, set off the floor about eighteen inches, so he had a good view of the room. The sergeant studied her curiously, one eyebrow raised, as she approached.

"Can I help you, miss?" he asked amiably enough.

"I hope so, Sergeant," she replied. "I'd like to speak to the detectives who caught the Meserve and Gage murders, if they're available."

Jenna didn't miss the tic of surprise on the man's face as he registered the confidence in her voice, and the certainty with which she noted his rank. Not to mention her use of the word *caught*. It was a cop term. A cop word, in this case.

But then he smiled. "You would, huh? Well, that'd be Detectives Grillo and Brody. You're out of luck at the moment, though. They *caught* another case this morning."

The sergeant studied Jenna as he spoke, obviously unsure what to make of her.

"Is there somewhere I can wait?" she asked.

With a small chuckle, the sergeant nodded. "Sure. Second floor, third door on the left is homicide. I'm sure there's someone around."

"Thank you."

Jenna turned and started for the stairs, moving around an officer who was escorting a shaggy man in handcuffs who was obviously drunk. She was halfway to the stairs when the sergeant called after her.

"Miss?"

When she glanced back, she saw that the amusement on his face had turned into a full-fledged grin.

"You watch too much television," he told her.

With a scowl, Jenna turned back toward the stairs,

both angry and embarrassed. Her familiarity with police procedure—or what little familiarity she had—didn't come from watching television, or the dozens of mystery novels she'd read. The sergeant's assumption that it had was bad enough, though, without the fact that he'd said it aloud in a room full of cops.

Upstairs, she quickly found the large office that housed the homicide unit. Jenna took a deep breath, trying to rid herself of the sour feeling created by the sergeant's comment, and entered. An older woman with a deeply lined face and steel gray hair sat behind a desk going through some files on her lap. Across the room, behind a glass partition, the office of the unit's lieutenant was empty. There was only one other person in the room, a short, thin, olive-skinned guy with a mustache, who peered over at Jenna with a mischievous glint in his eye.

The woman behind the desk didn't look up until Jenna cleared her throat.

"Can I help you?" she asked, obviously irked at having been interrupted at her task.

Jenna kept her expression impassive, staring directly into the woman's eyes. "I was told I could wait for Detectives Grillo and Brody in here."

"What's this regarding?" the woman asked, going back to the files in her lap.

"I wanted to talk to them about the Meserve and Gage murders."

The filing stopped. The woman glanced up at her again, this time much more closely, running some kind of instant appraisal on her. After a moment she gestured toward a nearby desk.

"That's Detective Grillo's desk," the woman said. "You can wait there. They're expected back shortly."

"Thank you."

Almost before she was seated in the metal-and-plastic chair next to Grillo's desk, the short guy strode across the room toward her. Everything about him seemed pleasant, from the warm expression on his face to the way he walked, as though at any moment he might begin to dance.

"Hi. You're waiting for Vic Grillo?"

"That's right." Jenna wanted to be on guard, in case this guy was as insulting as the sergeant downstairs. But he was so friendly and instantly charismatic, that she couldn't help but be won over.

"You might have to wait awhile," he told her. "Could another detective help you, perhaps, Miss . . . ?"

"Blake. Jenna Blake," she said, feeling absurdly formal as she held out her hand for him to shake. "And, no, I don't think so. Unless there's someone else I could talk to about the Meserve and Gage murders."

The little man's smile was speculative now.

"Huh. You know something about those murders, Miss Blake? Or are you just interested in one of the suspects' welfare?"

"I'm sorry," Jenna said hesitantly. "Are you a detective?"

The man seemed taken aback. Then he chuckled. "How rude of me. I'm sorry. My mother taught me better than that. I'm Aldo Donatello. I'm the lieutenant here."

Jenna couldn't hide her surprise. Though he seemed very smart and personable, Aldo Donatello didn't seem as imposing as she imagined someone in his position would have to be.

"I know, I don't really fit the bill, do I? I've got movies and TV to thank for that. Everybody expects the lieutenant to be Robert De Niro or something."

"Well, I was just told that I watch too much television, so I guess we're both victims," Jenna said.

Donatello laughed. "So, what can I do for you, Miss Blake?"

Jenna sighed. She was happy to have someone so ready to listen to her, but now that she did, she wasn't one hundred percent certain how to start.

"I . . . first I should say that I know it's none of my business, and I shouldn't be here, and it's not my job. And I'm sure you guys have everything under control anyway. But . . ." She paused and blushed a bit, feeling foolish. "I work for Walter Slikowski, he's the medical examiner for Suffolk County."

"How is Suffolk County involved?" Donatello asked quickly, all business suddenly.

"It isn't," Jenna explained. "I go to Somerset University, but I'm from Natick. I'm home for Christmas and, well, I went to high school with both of those guys, Chris and John, I mean. I just . . . was wondering if I could be of any help. I've helped out a lot with Dr. Slikowski on cases in Somerset and Cambridge, and—"

The lieutenant's eyebrows went up in amusement. Jenna was annoyed, and feeling more foolish than even the Cambridge cops had been able to make her feel. She thought about the things her friends had said the night before and wondered if they might not have been right.

"I appreciate the interest, and I'm sure if you have some insight, especially since you know the suspects, the detectives on the case will be happy to talk to you. But otherwise, well—"

"I know," she said quickly, trying to save herself further embarrassment. "That's not the way things work. I guess I just thought . . . I don't know what I thought."

Jenna stood and turned toward the door, feeling foolish.

"Miss Blake?"

Donatello caught up with her and touched her arm. "Why don't you sit back down? Like I said, I'm sure the detectives involved will be interested in what you have to"—his eyes darted toward the door—"and here they are now."

In the doorway stood an overweight, red-nosed, slovenly-looking detective who held a Dunkin' Donuts coffee cup in his hand. Behind him was another man, who looked a bit like David Duchovny in glasses. Donatello waved them over and introduced them. The coffee drinker was Mike Brody and his much neater partner was Vic Grillo.

Jenna stood, trying not to feel silly as Donatello explained what she was doing there. The detectives examined her with almost identical expressions of doubt. Then Donatello left her with them, and moments later Jenna found herself back in the chair next to Grillo's desk, with Brody leaning on the desk, drinking his coffee.

"Would you like some coffee?" Detective Grillo asked. "Or a soft drink? Anything?"

"I'm fine," Jenna replied, glancing at Brody's Dunkin' Donuts cup. "If you guys don't trust the coffee in here, neither do I."

That seemed to break the ice. Both detectives chuckled.

"So, Jenna," Grillo began, "you know the suspects? From high school? I know it's hard to believe that people you know could do something like this, but there's really no doubt."

She winced. That was what it was about, for them. It had nothing to do with whether or not she might have a sharp investigative mind, or even some intuition. They assumed she was there because she couldn't believe her friends were capable of horrible crimes.

With a sigh, Jenna rose from the seat.

"Know what? It was a mistake to come here," she said calmly. She smiled apologetically at the detectives. "You have a lot to do. I know that. Your lieutenant just told you that I work for the M.E. in Suffolk County. You look at me and you see a kid, and I understand that. Even if I were older, I've only been helping out on the M.E.'s cases for a few months. So you have no reason to listen to me."

"Who said we weren't gonna listen?" Brody asked, without looking up from his coffee cup.

Jenna didn't have an answer for that. A moment later, Brody did look up at her.

"We've got our suspects. Doesn't mean we're not trying to figure out why they did what they did. You got some insight into that, we're happy to hear it," Brody told her.

Which was when Jenna discovered something quite embarrassing.

"Y'know, I really don't," she confessed. "I guess I just came down to say that I know these guys. I can almost guarantee there was no death pact conspiracy or anything here. And the similarity of the two cases seems really suspicious to me."

"They led pretty similar lives," Detective Grillo said. "Plus, Gage could have been a copycat."

Frustrated, Jenna tried not to show it. "Maybe."

"You don't think so?" Brody asked.

"I think it's suspicious, that's all. The similarity. It makes me wonder if somebody else wasn't behind it, somehow making the guys do what they did."

"Like a mastermind or something?" Grillo asked doubtfully. "But you just said . . . I'm confused, now."

"I'm not saying I think they were in it together," she said. "Look, they both passed lie detector tests, right? Neither of them remembers doing anything. That's what the newspapers said."

The detectives exchanged a glance. It was Brody, the senior partner, who turned to her and nodded. "And?"

"I just think you should consider the possibility that someone was controlling them somehow."

"What, like *The Manchurian Candidate* or something?" Brody stared at her, waiting for an answer.

Jenna shook her head slowly. They thought she was some kind of freak or weirdo. Worse, the conversation had made her wonder if they weren't right to think that way.

"Thanks for your time," she said.

And she left.

The detectives made no effort to stop her.

Jenna stayed home that night. Her mother was at the hospital until well after dinnertime so she sat in the family room and surfed cable channels alone. After seven she made Annie's Shells and Cheddar from the box and sat on the couch to watch *Jeopardy!*

For the previous twenty-four hours—and in some ways, ever since she had come home—she had been struggling with the nostalgic temptation to perceive everything as unchanging. Herself included. All of her friends came home and expected everything to be just as they'd left it. Expected others to be just as they'd been before.

Jenna was guilty of it, and yet it had rankled in her mind from the moment she became aware of it. She was still the same person, sure. Jenna Blake, Natick kid, loves puzzles and books, plays a little piano—or did; she hadn't set her hands on one in ages. But she was also more than that, now. Every year, every bit added to a life was like a new wing built onto an old house.

But just as she didn't want Natick to change while she was away—she'd been upset to see that the old White Hen Pantry, where she'd bought candy as a girl, was now a Starbucks—her friends didn't want her to change, either.

Too late for that.

The only problem was, nobody was willing to see the changes in her. Nobody was willing to treat her like an adult. The cops had actually been a bit more cooperative than she might have expected, but they still didn't believe that she might have anything to contribute. In retrospect, Jenna honestly couldn't blame them. She was eighteen, and she sometimes looked younger.

But they shouldn't just dismiss me out of hand, she thought now. *At least give me a chance to help.*

She sighed and dug into her bowl of shells and cheese. The pepper she had sprinkled over it added just the right flavor. If she followed it up with a good salad, it would probably be a better dinner than her mom would end up having.

With a sigh, Jenna reached for the remote control. *Jeopardy!* had ended, and she was ready to start surfing again. She hoped that her mother would come home soon. She'd have someone to talk to, or at the very least, she'd have her mother there to sit with her and watch television.

That's what she needed at the moment: her mom. Since nobody seemed to want to let her grow up,

Jenna had determined that she would do the opposite. With her sweatpants on and the remote in her hand and a bowl of Annie's in front of her, she felt a lot more like the Jenna of eighth grade than anything else. She thought about the posters and stuffed animals and things in her bedroom, and found that she was glad they were there.

Being a "grown-up" could really suck. Jenna decided that it was okay to be a kid again, just for a little while.

If you can't beat 'em, join 'em, she thought.

An hour or so later April finally came home. With one look, Jenna could see how exhausted her mother was. All day on her feet, not to mention however many surgeries she had performed that day, checking in on her patients, maybe some administrative meetings—it wasn't an easy job.

So when April came out of her bedroom in a flannel nightshirt and thick wool socks, Jenna made room on the sofa, and they watched George Clooney in *Out of Sight* on cable and agreed wholeheartedly that he was "yummy."

At first April only looked at Jenna. Then she nodded, a sly smile on her face. "I've never called a man 'yummy' in my life, but if I'm going to start, it would have to be George."

"You just love him 'cause he used to be Dr. Ross. I love George the man. He's totally mine, and you can just back off," Jenna said, one eyebrow arched.

"*You* have a boyfriend, little girl."

Jenna pouted. "Got me there." Then her mind was

sidetracked. She had meant to call Damon down in Florida earlier, but she just hadn't been in the mood to talk to anyone. Now it was too late, and she'd have to talk to him in the morning.

"So," her mother said, interrupting her train of thought. "Want to tell me what's got you so down?"

For a moment Jenna was tempted to ask her mother how she knew anything at all was bothering her. But she already knew what April would say: "I'm your mother."

Feeling a bit foolish, Jenna told her about the trip to the police station that day. April listened patiently and frowned in all the right places. When Jenna was done, her mother was thoughtful for a minute.

"They should have taken you more seriously," April told her. "But you also have to try to see things from their perspective."

"I know." Jenna sighed. "I'm a kid."

April laughed and reached out to mess up her daughter's hair. "Yeah, you're a kid," she said. "Still a kid, though you think you're all grown up now because you're living on your own and you have this job. But that's not the point."

"What *is* the point, then?"

"They don't know you, Jenna," April said softly. "Dr. Slikowski, the other people you work with, even the police officers you've worked with . . . they know who you are. You proved you could handle all this stuff right from the start.

"Of course, I'm your mom. I know you can do it. I believe in you, Jenna. Always have, always will. You can do anything that you set your mind to, no doubt about that. These local cops, they don't know you well enough to see past that cute college co-ed exterior."

Jenna laughed. "Who the hell says 'co-ed' anymore?" she teased.

"Hey, I'm old, give me a break, will ya?"

"You're not that old," Jenna told her. "In fact, I bet George would think you're a total hottie."

"Damn straight," April agreed.

They sat together, leaning on each other, and turned their attention back to the movie. Fifteen minutes shy of the climax, April's breathing deepened, and Jenna glanced sidelong at her, not at all surprised to find that her mother had fallen asleep. When the movie was over, she got up and let April have the sofa to herself. She stretched out there, and Jenna figured that's where she'd find her mother in the morning. It would hardly be the first time.

Before she turned in herself, she bent to kiss her mother's forehead.

"Thanks," she whispered. "I love you."

Three miles away, on the far south side of Natick, Alisa Farmer stood looking down at her father, who had fallen asleep in his reclining chair, ESPN droning endlessly in the background. Three scotch-and-sodas—Al Farmer's usual Friday night intake—made him a very sound sleeper.

He hadn't heard Alisa come up from the basement, where the old tiled playroom they'd built in the seventies had been converted to include her home-from-college sleeping quarters. She and her little sister had been down there watching movies, or something, last he knew.

But the last he knew was after the first drink.

There had been a scuffle downstairs, but that hadn't woken him either.

In the large bedroom at the end of the hall on the split-level's second floor, Marjorie Farmer was also asleep, with the Home and Garden network on. With that as background noise, Marjorie also had not been roused by the sound of the scuffle downstairs.

In the basement playroom, the tiles were spattered in some places—and literally weeping and pooling in others—with the blood of Janine Farmer. There was a long screwdriver in her right hand.

Al had left his tool box open on a table in the basement. When the two girls watched the videotape together, they had both felt the sudden urge to attack. To grab weapons. To draw blood.

The Farmer girls—known locally and with much amusement as "Farmer's daughters," savaged one another in a joint, vicious attack. Alisa had a ballpeen hammer. Janine had a long screwdriver, which she drove into her sister's abdomen and thigh.

But when the outbreak of horrid violence was over, Janine lay dead, beaten to death with the hammer. When Alisa went upstairs, she was bleeding profusely from her wounds. The blood soaked the front of her clothes and left a red trail in her wake as she moved around the house, still wielding the hammer.

Alisa examined the hammer, grinning at the reflection of her face in steel. Then she turned from the sleeping, snoring form of her father and went swiftly and silently down the hall to her mother's room. Dad was going to sleep through it all, she thought.

Well, not all . . .

Still, she decided to go to her mother's room next, and save Dad for last.

chapter 9

"This is what I get for going away for the holidays."

Danny Mariano stood in the coffee room at the headquarters of the Somerset Police Department, blowing the steam off his coffee cup. He shook his head in consternation.

His partner, Audrey Gaines, offered a rare smile, amused by his complaints. "Hey, nobody told your mother to move to Florida, Danny. Not to mention that, frankly, the idea of spending Christmas down on the beach with the sun and surf is pretty revolting. We had a white Christmas this year, by the way."

"Don't remind me," Danny grumbled.

His father had died several years earlier, and his mother had moved to Fort Myers Beach. At the time, she had promised to spend Christmas in New England with him every year. But this year, to his frustration, she hadn't felt like flying. Which meant Christmas in Florida.

Danny loved Christmas. Everything about it. The music, the lights, the trees, the presents, the mistletoe. But part of Christmas for him was always going to be the New England weather. Christmas was supposed to be cold; if God could manage a little snow for the holiday, so much the better.

"Some of us worked on Christmas day, partner," Audrey said gruffly. "Don't complain."

Danny smiled at that. But he stopped complaining. He sipped at his coffee and counted his blessings. With the murder of the mayor, Somerset had fallen apart while he was out of town, and Danny was content to have missed the chaos. Now, though, he was part of the cleanup team—not an easy job.

"How many calls did you get from reporters today?" he asked Audrey.

"Not as many as yesterday." She poured a package of cocoa mix into a cup of hot water, then added milk and sugar and stirred it up. It wasn't exactly real hot chocolate, but it wasn't just hot water, either. When she lifted the cup to her lips and tasted it, she grimaced, but didn't put it back down.

"They've been at it long enough that they know we've got nothing we're willing to give them. At least until something new comes up," she explained.

"Yeah," Danny agreed. "They've reached the point now where they're just making it up as they go along."

"So are we," Audrey reminded him. "But at least we've got a fresh perspective."

Sergeant Bellamy poked her head into the coffee

room, looking harried as always. "The M.E.'s here, Detectives. He's been waiting. Also, a woman named Maureen Marchese just showed up. Says you asked her to come down."

Audrey's eyebrows went up. "Talk about timing."

Danny nodded. "Thanks, Claire."

The sergeant nodded, and then she was gone.

"You're way ahead of me on this case, Audrey," he began.

"I'll take Marchese. You and Walter can watch from the observation room. If I miss anything, come on in."

Audrey took another sip from her cup, wrinkled her nose, and then tossed the whole thing into the big trash can in the corner. She went out into the squad room, and Danny followed. Beyond the reception desk in the homicide unit's large bullpen office sat a woman with raven hair and a face like a porcelain doll. Her skin was white and her eyes large and damp, as though she spent her life on the verge of tears. She wore a neatly tailored, dark green suit.

Instantly, Danny wanted to help her. Not a good way for a cop to feel about a suspect in an ongoing murder investigation, but there it was. He couldn't help it.

Maybe it's a good thing Audrey's doing the interview, he thought.

On the other side of the room, next to Danny's desk, Dr. Slikowski sat in his wheelchair, looking a bit bored and a lot impatient. It was unlike the M.E. to be so blatant about such things, but as Danny walked toward him, he caught Slick glancing at his watch.

"Got a hot date?" he asked quietly as he slipped into his chair.

Slick frowned. "If you consider an autopsy a hot date, Detective, then yes. I have two of them this afternoon."

"I love Monday," Danny replied.

Out of the corner of his eye, he saw Audrey escorting the Marchese woman into Interview Two. As soon as the door was closed, he dropped the relaxed attitude he'd adopted with Slick.

"Sorry about that, Walter," he said quickly, already standing. "I just didn't want to talk about the case in front of a suspect. My condolences on the mayor's death. Audrey tells me you were friends. I saw a bit about the funeral on the news last night."

The M.E. nodded. "It was a circus. The politician in Jim would've loved it, but it was hard on his family. That was Maureen Marchese, then, that Audrey just took into the interview room?"

"That's right. We thought you might want to observe, which is why she called you this morning."

Slick nodded slowly. "Yes, of course. Sorry if I seemed impatient."

"No harm, no foul. Let's go."

Danny felt the momentary urge to push Slick's wheelchair along, but resisted the temptation. He'd gotten the sense that the man hated to have his chair pushed by anyone if he could avoid it. It was an odd sensation for Danny.

The only times he'd ever pushed anyone in a wheelchair were when fooling around with his friends or trundling his aging grandmother through Disney World as a child. But Walter Slikowski's personality was so powerful, his manner so strong and confident, that it was easy to forget that he wasn't just in the chair as a lark, or because he was tired.

He didn't have the use of his legs.

Danny walked beside him to the door of the observation room, then stood aside and let the M.E. enter before him. They stared together through the one-way glass on the wall. Inside the interview room it looked like a mirror. Anyone on the inside who had ever seen a police show on television would know, or at least guess, that there were people watching from the other side. That wasn't always true, but since the glass was one-way, nobody in the interview room could ever be certain if they were being watched or not.

Of course, people who weren't actually being interrogated—who instead had been asked to come down just to "talk," as Maureen Marchese had been—would probably assume that nobody was watching through the mirror.

Even so, when Audrey and Marchese sat down across the metal table from each other, Marchese frowned at the mirror. Danny felt strange, as though she knew he was there. It was an odd sensation.

Maureen Marchese didn't cut the figure of a faceless, coldhearted bureaucrat. There was nothing remotely stiff or stern about her. She was more kindly grade school teacher than politician. But she was also scared. Danny could see that right off.

"Miss Marchese seems a bit nervous, doesn't she?" Slick asked.

Danny glanced at the M.E. Slick removed his wire-rim glasses and cleaned them on the white button-down shirt he wore. When he looked up again, Danny saw the shadows under his eyes, the dark circles that told a great deal about how *his* holidays had been.

For a moment Danny considered not speaking the next words that came into his head. But he did.

"Most of the time—not implying anything here—but most of the time, someone in politics gets shot or drowned or thrown off a building, it turns out they were maybe not as good as everyone thought they were. Kerchak was your friend. How sure can you be that isn't the case here?"

Slick stiffened, his upper body rigid against the back of the wheelchair. But he didn't look at Danny again.

"There have been times, Detective, when good men have been killed simply for being what they are."

Danny nodded slowly. He tried to think of something to say, something to smooth over the rough spot he'd just created, but nothing came to mind. *And maybe it's better that way,* he thought. *Quit while you're behind, Mariano.*

The two men listened to the conversation through an intercom system that filtered sound from Interview Two into the observation room. Audrey had settled Maureen Marchese down with soothing words and a can of Diet Coke. As he watched and listened, Danny started to forget about Dr. Slikowski and whether or not he had offended the man.

Maureen Marchese captured all of his attention.

Danny narrowed his eyes. It wasn't just that she was beautiful, which she was in an odd way, sort of like Christina Ricci at forty. There was something tragic about her every gesture. Maureen Marchese was damaged goods, and it didn't sit right with him.

"Look, Maureen," Audrey was saying, "let me get down to business, here. We have new evidence that supports an earlier time of death for Mayor Kerchak."

"That's impossible," Marchese said in a jittery voice. "I was there until late; our meeting didn't get over until—"

"I know that," Audrey said calmly, comfortingly. "Maureen, where was this meeting?"

"In . . . in the mayor's office," Marchese replied.

Lie. Danny could hear it in her voice. Almost like she didn't care anymore if they knew she was lying. But there was something going on here, and he trusted Audrey to coax it out of the woman. After all, she'd taught him everything he knew about handling an interview.

"You're the city's director of development, Maureen. You handle contracts and permits, the city's new construction enterprises. There are a lot of people who make a lot of money in those businesses. Some of them don't do it honestly. Some of them are pretty much lowlifes. Ever come into contact with that element in your job, Maureen?"

"Of course," Marchese replied, with a flutter of her right hand. She touched her temple, as though she might be getting a headache.

"What time did you leave City Hall the night the mayor was killed?"

"Before nine o'clock," she replied, meeting Audrey's gaze.

Danny thought Maureen Marchese looked like a deer caught in the headlights of an onrushing car. Frozen in those lights. Oddly, he remembered a book he'd read—*Watership Down*—in which the author talked about animals doing just that. *Going tharn*, that was how the animals thought of it. Their word.

Maureen Marchese had gone tharn.

"Jim Kerchak wasn't killed on the roof, Maureen," Audrey said, and Marchese winced as if Audrey had said something particularly filthy. "Not only was he murdered much earlier than we'd originally thought, but he was murdered inside the building.

"Where was the meeting you had with the mayor, Maureen?"

Danny watched, entranced. They had no proof that the meeting had been in Marchese's office, or that the mayor had been killed there. The crime scene guys hadn't come up with anything conclusive. But given that she was the last person in the building, the last to see the mayor alive, and Slick's very reasonable ideas about the mayor having been killed inside the building . . . well, letting her believe they knew just what had happened might lead her to share the truth with them.

And she knew that truth; of that much, Danny was certain.

"Maureen?" Audrey prodded.

Not too hard, Danny mentally chided.

Then Maureen Marchese began to shudder, and hot tears sprang to her eyes and stained her cheeks. Audrey didn't move to comfort her; instead, she just waited. Marchese wiped tears from her eyes, her features contorted with the pain of her emotions.

"I'm so . . . so afraid," she whispered, her voice barely a croak.

"What are you afraid of, Maureen?" Audrey asked.

"They said I'd be next. That they'd do the same to me if I said anything. I've been so afraid. I haven't slept a whole night since . . . then."

"We're going to take care of you, Maureen," Audrey said. "We'll make sure nobody hurts you. But you've got to cooperate. The best way to protect yourself is to get the people responsible for this off the street."

Marchese laughed. It was a tragic sound. "Good luck," she said. "The FBI's been trying to put Frank Schiavelli away for twenty years."

Danny recoiled. Behind that one-way glass, he marveled at how well Audrey managed to keep her composure. Beside him, Dr. Slikowski actually swore under his breath. He didn't think he'd ever heard Slick use a curse word before. Any other day it would have been funny.

"You're saying Frank Schiavelli killed the mayor?" Audrey asked, her words clipped.

"No," Marchese replied. "I'm saying some big, ugly grunt named Tino killed Jim Kerchak, while Schiavelli stood and watched him do it. In the middle of my office."

She lost it then, sobbing uncontrollably. "All I . . . could do . . . was watch."

"Oh, my God," Danny whispered.

Jenna wasn't getting anywhere.

For the better part of two days, she had been attempting to get a lead on what might have caused her former classmates to do the things they had done. The news that Alisa Farmer had murdered her family had been horrifying, but not really much of a shock.

If anybody had bothered to ask her, Jenna could have predicted that it wasn't over.

More to the point, she had never really known Alisa that well. She didn't remember if they'd ever actually spoken in high school. However, the murders of the Farmer family did change the landscape of the case somewhat. The killers weren't all male. They weren't all friends.

But they had all graduated from Natick High in the same year.

There had to be more than that, but for now, it was all she had to go on. With the families of the killers all dead, Jenna didn't know where to start. Her friends had not been very supportive, and though she'd received a lot of moral support from Damon by phone and Yoshiko by e-mail, neither of them was around. Nor did she think they could do much to help her if they were.

If only the cops would let me in on the investigation, she thought. But that was a useless avenue to go down. *I'm on my own.*

She sat now at a table at the California Pizza Kitchen in Natick Mall, across from another person she'd rarely, if ever, spoken to in high school. In this case, however, it was because Todd Gage almost never spoke. He was John's second cousin and best friend, and had graduated from Natick High along with everyone else, though he was a year younger.

Todd was as brilliant as he was quiet. High school had taken him three years instead of four. College was likely to be even shorter. He'd gotten a free ride to Yale, and anywhere else he would have wanted to go. It hadn't been easy to get him talking. In fact, Jenna thought the only reason he was willing to talk to her at all was because he remembered that she and John had been friendly.

"He didn't do this," Todd insisted, for perhaps the fourth time.

Jenna chewed her lip a moment. "Todd. You're going to go to law school. I care about John, so I'd rather not say this, but I think you'll find the evidence is pretty damning."

Before Todd could protest, Jenna held up a hand. "Bear with me a second. I think there are way too many similarities in the Farmer and Meserve cases. I can't believe that's coincidental. I'd be willing to bet that they were all exposed to the same influence—something that would actually alter their behavior, be it chemical or whatever. If I'm right, the big question is, was it accidental, or did someone do it to them on purpose, manipulate them somehow? I could play it coy and ask you questions like I'm some kind of detective. I'm not. I'm just trying to find out what happened here."

Todd let that sink in. After a moment, he looked at her with his brow furrowed. "Manipulated how?"

"I don't know," she confessed. "I was hoping you could help me with that. John was your best friend—"

"Is. He *is* my best friend."

"I'm sorry. I know that. I'm not . . . it's important that you remember that I'm not a cop. But I have to ask . . . I mean, I know John got high sometimes. I've seen him. I'm not passing judgment. What I'm wondering is if he did anything out of the ordinary. Pills? Anything new?"

Jenna was relieved to see that instead of being offended, Todd was really thinking about it. She understood why. Her line of questioning was an attempt to establish a real defense for John. She was only grateful that Todd was perceptive enough to see that.

"I wish I could help you," he said at last, shrugging his shoulders.

"Did he seem strange to you, at all? I mean, the last few days before Christmas."

"We've both been away at school. He seemed a little different, but not in any weird way. Just . . . we've got our own lives now, you know?"

Jenna thought of Priya and Moira and nodded. "I do know."

"I have to say, though, he seemed fine. Happy. I saw him Christmas day, and everything was great. We just hung out and did the usual things, talked about what we'd gotten for Christmas. It was like we were ten years old again or something. But John's always that way at Christmas. He . . ."

Todd's words trailed off. Jenna knew what must have been going through his head. It didn't seem likely that John's childlike love for Christmas would survive this tragedy. Even if there was something the police had missed, even if John somehow miraculously managed to avoid going to jail, Christmas would be a time of despair for him all his life.

Jenna took a breath. It was so difficult for her to separate her feelings from her desire to help. But she had to.

"Thanks, Todd," she said. "If you think of anything—"

"I'll let you know," he promised. "One thing I will say, though."

Jenna studied him curiously.

"The last day or so, the media's been starting to turn this thing into one of those crusades against violence on TV and in video games, or whatever. Well John hasn't played a video game since junior high, as far as I know. And I hung out with Alisa Farmer a bit in high school. I don't think she *ever* played them."

Jenna considered that. Todd confirmed what she had believed from the start. The police, and now the media, were trying to find the truth, or at least some kind of link to bring them around to it. Three promising young people all snapping within a handful of days, murdering their families. They couldn't make sense of it, couldn't see a connection. They were all searching for one, scrambling to find some explanation. Video games were handy.

Not to mention trendy.

If all they wanted to do was point to the easiest scapegoat, they could pick anything from Internet chat rooms to the popularity of professional wrestling. It was idiotic, Jenna thought. She knew there was something they were missing. Something *she* was missing. And she was determined to figure out what it was.

When she got home, there was a message from Dr. Slikowski. He was checking up on her, inquiring as to how things had been going with the murders in Natick. He also said that there had been some progress in the investigation of the mayor's murder. His voice on the answering machine was quite tentative, and she assumed it was because he couldn't really tell her much.

Jenna thought it had been very nice of him to check up on her. She was also grateful because she was frustrated, feeling as though she hadn't been getting anywhere at all. If the Natick cops had been more cooperative . . .

It occurred to her, suddenly, that she could ask Slick to get involved, to try to use whatever influence he had to get them to take her more seriously. Almost instantly she rejected the idea. At the end of the day, she was still just some kid halfway through her freshman year in college. Even if they acted as though they were going to take her seriously, that didn't mean they would.

Jenna sighed. She and Slick made an excellent team. The progress in the Kerchak investigation proved that.

They were like the dynamic duo or something. Things just went more smoothly when they were working together.

When you've got an official reason to stick your nose in, you mean, she thought.

It made her smile. Yet another reason she longed to get back to school. If the Natick cops didn't want her help, so be it. But that didn't mean she was going to stop searching for answers.

It hadn't turned out at all the way he'd planned.

Three. Only three.

The visitor who had delivered unwanted and dangerous presents to a great many people in Natick just before Christmas sat now in front of his computer and his audiovisual equipment and raged with frustration. There had been over two dozen tapes delivered, and he had expected a success ratio of fifty to sixty percent. All of his long-term forecasts had indicated those numbers to be accurate.

But three? That was only twelve or thirteen percent.

It would never do.

Though he knew it might take him as long as six months to go over every inch of that tape and do his calculations again, he didn't have a choice. There was a bright side to all of this. He had proven that he could do it. The people he wanted to impress would have to see that.

But if he couldn't manage better results than thirteen percent . . . well, he didn't have a choice. He'd have to start again.

On the other hand, he thought, *it's early. Some of them might not have even watched the tape yet.*

He decided to give it another week before making any rash judgments. It was the holiday season, after all. If he was going back to the drawing board, he thought he deserved a few more days of relaxation first.

At a quarter past six on Monday night, Walter rode the elevator up from the basement of Somerset Medical Center. After spending the morning at the police station and then performing two autopsies with the barely adequate assistance of a surgery resident named Carl Hanulcik, he was completely exhausted. When the elevator reached the second floor, Walter rolled his wheelchair down the corridor in particularly lethargic fashion.

He didn't realize the time until he reached the T junction in the hall and turned down toward his office. At the end of that short corridor, Natalie Kerchak sat on the floor with her nose in a book, her red hair pulled up and away from her face with some kind of clip.

"Oh, Natalie," he whispered.

There were no recriminations. She didn't say, "Walter, you're late," or any variation thereof. She only smiled patiently and slipped a leather bookmark into her book, which she then dropped into her purse.

"I'm sorry," he said as he propelled himself tiredly toward her. "I should have sent someone up to tell you I was . . . How late am I, exactly?"

Natalie held out her wrist so that he could see her watch. He'd promised to meet her at six to take her out to dinner, and now he was going on twenty minutes late.

"I really am sorry." Walter fumbled in his pocket for the key card that would let him into the office.

Natalie didn't say anything as they went inside the office and Walter turned on the lights.

"Let me just see if there are any urgent messages, and then we can get going," he said, feeling a bit flushed with regret and embarrassment. This lateness, the way his job superseded all else, had been one of the reasons things hadn't worked out between them, back when.

"Take your time," Natalie said, a profound affection in her voice.

At the door to his inner office, Walter turned to look at her curiously. "I'm sorry if I'm staring," he said, unable to keep the irony out of his voice. "It's just that I don't recall ever hearing you use that particular phrase before."

Her eyes narrowed. "Don't push your luck, Walter." Then a kind of wry smile graced her features, and a sadness descended upon her eyes. When she spoke again, it was in a whisper.

"Jim and I weren't always the closest of siblings, but

he was a good brother. I miss him more than I ever imagined I would. It's strange, really. I thought that whichever of us died first, the other would grieve mostly for the children we once were. The things we did. The fun and the fights and all of that. But now . . ." She faltered, looked away.

"Now I miss the man. Jim was a good man, Walter. The older I get the more I recognize the value and scarcity of a good man. He was my brother, and I miss him, and I want to see whoever is responsible for it pay dearly. You're working for that, and I appreciate it."

Natalie approached him, crouched down before him in a manner that would have made him self-conscious, like a child being reprimanded, if it had been anyone else. Her hand fluttered in the air and she touched his cheek with the backs of her fingers.

"I'm seeing what you do from the other side now. From the side everyone hopes never to be on. If your being late means you were trying to do for other people what you're trying to do for me and for my brother's family . . . well, I think I've got to allow for a little absentmindedness here and there. It's called a new perspective. I just wish I had seen it a long time ago, before the part of my story that has you in it had drifted so far away."

Walter was silent as she spoke, the effect of her fingers touching his face electric. He smiled gently.

"That's very poetic," he said sincerely. "But I have to correct you. From what I can see, the part of your story that has me in it isn't completely over yet."

"No," she said, pleasantly surprised by his response. "I suppose it isn't."

Her mouth moved toward his, and their lips met in a soft kiss. It was brief, but when Natalie withdrew, Walter did not pursue her for another. There was a great deal unresolved about their feelings. But given her current emotional state, and the news he had to discuss with her that evening, he knew that such resolutions would have to wait.

Perhaps forever.

With a pleasant buzz from Natalie's attentions working through him, Walter went into his office and checked the messages on his voice mail.

"Hi, Dr. Slikowski, it's Jenna. I guess I'll try to catch up with you tomorrow. Sounds like you've got good news. Wish I could say the same. I'd like to help with all the chaos here, but I'm getting the cold shoulder from the local homicide guys." There was a pause, as if she were rethinking her words. "Anyway . . . talk to you later."

Walter considered calling her back—there was a frustration in her tone that made him want to help—but he had already kept Natalie waiting long enough, and he decided to call Jenna in the morning. There were several other messages, but nothing terribly urgent, so he grabbed his jacket from the low hook on the coat rack and went out to join Natalie.

It was a crisp evening, the sky clear but holding the vaguest whispered promise of snow. Walter could smell it coming. His brother had always argued with him, telling him it was ridiculous, that one could not smell an oncoming storm, be it rain or snow. Walter disagreed. He was not a man with a lot of eccentric or erroneous beliefs. Aliens and auras and psychic powers weren't within the parameters of his personal system of logic.

But it was going to snow soon. That much he knew. He could smell it.

He drove them to the North End of Boston in his van, and they had dinner at a tiny Italian restaurant on Prince Street called Asaggio. The veal saltimbocca was particularly delicious, though Natalie made the usual protests about his eating veal. It was an argument he preferred to avoid, and he did so deftly, discussing instead her taste for antiques and the latest jazz offerings he had ordered off the Internet.

They talked about her life, the children's charity she did volunteer work for, and the seemingly endless construction in and around the city of Boston. By the time they were working on their dessert, a fine example of tiramisu that they shared, Walter had begun to feel guilty. He had been enjoying the evening and her company so much that he had put off giving her the news about her brother's murder quite on purpose.

When the tiramisu was gone, and they sat together, he sipping his tea and she drinking strong coffee with great contentment, Walter regarded her with a grave set to his features. Natalie noticed almost instantly.

"What is it?"

"I ought to have told you this sooner," he admitted. "I was waiting for an appropriate moment, but I should have spoken up before. There have been some significant developments in the investigation into Jim's death."

Natalie shook her head as if she hadn't understood. "What? What's happened?"

He took a breath, then pressed on. "The police have a witness."

"A witness. To Jim's murder? Someone who actually saw it happen?" she asked incredulously. "And you didn't think this was important enough to tell me when I got to your office earlier?"

"Selfish, I know," he said. "I thought I'd tell you when we got here, but you seemed so happy, I thought—"

Natalie sighed. "You thought right," she said. "You probably should have told me, but I'm glad you didn't. It was nice just to . . ." She let her words trail off, and then gave the slightest shake of her head. "Anyway, go on. What've they got?"

"Maureen Marchese, the director of development for the city, was accepting bribes from Frank Schiavelli."

Natalie frowned. "The mob guy? I don't get it."

"Construction projects, trucking, land deals . . . you name it," Walter said. "Anything the city was involved in, Marchese had to sign off on. Schiavelli was paying for favoritism."

"So Jim . . ." Natalie swallowed hard, her eyes growing damp. "Jim found out about it, and they killed him for it?"

Walter leaned back slightly in his wheelchair. "Miss Marchese got scared. She told your brother. He told her he'd back her up if she testified, brought Schiavelli down. It would have meant her job, but that was preferable to her than to continue doing what she had been doing. Apparently Schiavelli realized she was having a change of heart, because he and two other men went to City Hall to threaten Maureen. They knew she was working late, but they didn't expect to find her with the mayor."

Walter's voice dropped to just above a whisper. He reached across the table and took Natalie's hands in his. Her eyes were wide, haunted. She looked lost. There was the slightest hesitation in his voice. It was one thing to have someone you love murdered. It was something else to discover why and how it had been done, and to know that the reason was so crass. He rarely got this close to the fallout from his job, and it affected him profoundly.

"There was an argument. Maureen refused to cooperate any further. Schiavelli tried to buy Jim's silence, but he wanted nothing to do with it. He actually picked up the phone to call the police. That was when they killed him. Schiavelli and one of his thugs. Schiavelli told Maureen she would be considered an accomplice if she talked, but if that didn't scare her, he'd kill her as easily as he murdered Jim. She was terrified, of course. Schiavelli had killed the mayor; he'd think nothing of murdering her. When she left, they were still there. She's been living in terror ever since."

Natalie's eyes grew cold. "Good," she grunted.

Walter looked away. He was tempted to tell her that

she couldn't blame Maureen Marchese for Jim's murder, but he didn't dare. He understood.

Once upon a time, Walter Slikowski had been in Natalie's position, trying to find someone to blame for the murder of someone he'd loved; that and more. He wasn't about to pass judgment on her feelings, or her rationality.

"So what now?" she asked.

"Miss Marchese goes into protective custody. The D.A. puts together the warrants, and they arrest Frank Schiavelli. Probably as early as tomorrow afternoon."

"You'll keep me posted?"

"Of course."

Natalie gazed at the flickering light of the candle on their table as though she'd been hypnotized. Finally, she looked up at Walter grimly.

"I'm glad you didn't tell me before, I guess. But don't do that again, okay?"

"Okay."

"You want to walk around a bit?" she asked. "It's cold, but I think I need to clear my head."

Another time he might have joked with her, pointing out that much as he'd like to, he was incapable of walking around with her. Tonight, he merely nodded. After the bill had been paid, they went out into the narrow maze of streets that made up Boston's North End and wandered together, without speaking, for quite some time.

"Coffee?"

Danny felt like hell, and he pretty much figured he

looked the way he felt. After the revelation that one of Boston's top mafiosi was involved in Jim Kerchak's murder, he'd spent most of the night with all the files and newspaper stories related to Schiavelli that he could get his hands on. The FBI and Boston P.D. had been trying to take Schiavelli for a long time, but he was too slick. Always had a fall guy.

"Danny?" Audrey prodded.

He glanced at her, and was heartened to see that she didn't look much better than he did. She had her own copies of the files he was reading. It surprised Danny a little. Audrey was usually so up on current events that she didn't need to do her homework. *Maybe it was a refresher course for her,* he thought.

"Huh?"

"Coffee?" she asked again.

"Yeah. Lots. Buckets. Much sugar." He rubbed his bleary, red-rimmed eyes.

"You're supercop today, partner," Audrey said sarcastically. "Let's try to keep you inside so no one gets accidentally shot."

"I feel hungover," he replied, not rising to her taunts. "I only wish I'd been able to get nice and buzzed to earn the feeling."

Then his mind was wandering, working something over in his head the way a bee bangs against a closed window trying to get out.

"What's on your mind?" Audrey asked, when she noticed that his demeanor wasn't just from exhaustion.

Danny sighed. Shrugged. Scratched his head.

"Hello?" Audrey snapped.

She'd never been very patient.

"It's nothing, really," he said. "Kind of morbid. I just can't understand why a guy as smooth as Schiavelli, a guy nobody can ever pin anything significant on, would let Maureen Marchese live. I mean, he was there. She can put him there, on the stand; tell the jury he ordered Kerchak's murder. And he let her walk away.

"Why?"

Audrey tilted her head and regarded him. "I wondered the same thing. In fact I've been doing a little poking around. I was just going to fill you in."

Danny nodded. "So?"

"Marchese gets a free ride from the D.A. on all the influence-peddling charges. She's already been deposed regarding the murder. We'll bring in the goon Schiavelli had actually kill the mayor, turn him over with a promise of leniency. Then we'll have Marchese's deposition and the mook's testimony, enough to put Schiavelli away, and we can still put Marchese away on murder charges as an accomplice."

"The FBI will be very happy," Danny said bitterly.

The feds had been working the case a very long time. It was bound to be their bust.

"Actually," Audrey said, "they're going to share credit."

"You're kidding."

"I'm getting coffee," Audrey announced.

As she walked away, Danny turned that one over in his head. The FBI wasn't the ogre of an agency a lot of movies made them out to be, but they did like to get the blue ribbon whenever possible. They didn't have to share credit on this one. He was happy they had decided to do that.

On the other hand, Boston P.D. would be pissed. Danny smiled again.

The phone rang and he picked it up.

"Homicide. Detective Mariano."

"Danny, it's Walter Slikowski."

"Dr. Slikowski, I'm glad you called," he said. "We've got a meeting this afternoon with the FBI investigative team working the Schiavelli case. They asked if you could join us, I guess to explain how you came to establish the time of death, location, and all of that. It's in your autopsy report—or most of it is— but I figured you might be interested anyway. I know the mayor was a friend."

"I am, Danny. Thank you. What time is the meeting?"

"Three-thirty, if that's all right with you."

"I'll be there," the M.E. confirmed. "There was something else, though. I wanted to talk to you about Jenna Blake."

Danny frowned. Though she was much younger than he was, there had been a time, several months earlier, when Jenna had shown a real interest in him. Her interest wasn't one-sided. But Danny knew that any involvement with an eighteen-year-old college girl would not look good to his superiors, and there was a part of him that thought it was just a little strange. He hoped that the M.E. didn't think there was anything happening there.

"Okay. What about Jenna? Is she all right?"

"Well, I know she thinks of you as a friend, and I presume the feeling's mutual," Slick began. "She's home for the holidays, as you may know, and has become involved with an investigation there. You may have seen the pieces on the news about the teenagers who killed their families. It's been fairly omnipresent these last few days."

"How could I miss it?" he replied, thinking of the saturation coverage the case had been receiving. Between the Natick family killings and Jim Kerchak's murder, there'd barely been any room for other news. "What's Jenna's involvement?"

"Not as much as she'd like, actually," Slick confided. "The three suspects were high school classmates of hers. She believes there's more to the killings than meets the eye, but the Natick P.D. don't seem willing to take her seriously."

Audrey came back and handed Danny a large cup of coffee. He nodded his thanks.

"You think if I reached out to them, vouched for her, maybe they'd stop giving her the brush-off?"

"It couldn't hurt," Slick replied.

"Let me see what I can do," Danny said.

After he hung up, he drank about half his coffee in half a minute. It was hot, but not so hot that he couldn't gulp it down greedily. It wasn't very good, but not the usual swill, either. And unless some joker had replaced the real thing with decaf as a gag, it would be like mainlining caffeine.

Addiction was so tragic, but this morning, a necessary evil.

"What's up?" Audrey asked.

He explained what Slick had told him. Audrey raised an eyebrow and smiled thinly, but said nothing. While he and Jenna had flirted around the possibility of some kind of involvement, Audrey had made her disapproval very clear. It was obvious she still thought he should steer clear of her.

"It's just a favor for a friend," he told her, exasperated.

"So was Marilyn Monroe singing 'Happy Birthday' to Kennedy," she said with a cynical laugh.

Danny rolled his eyes as he picked up the phone. A few minutes later, he had a lieutenant named Aldo Donatello on the line.

"Yeah, I remember the girl," he said. "What's your interest, Detective?"

"Actually, Lieutenant Donatello, I just thought I'd give you a call and tell you she's stand-up. She's young, yeah, but she's been working with the M.E. here the last few months, and she's been a key player in a couple of investigations. She's a smart kid."

Donatello took his time replying. "This girl ask you to call?" he said finally.

"Not at all, Lieutenant," Danny told him. "I just heard from a friend that she was in the middle of this thing you've got going out there. I wouldn't say it to her, sir, 'cause I wouldn't want her to get a swelled head, but she's not like other kids her age. She just sees things differently. If she weren't planning to go into forensics, I'd be trying to convince her to come on the job."

"She's still a civilian, Detective," Donatello said.

"Yes, sir," Danny agreed. "But she's sharper than most veteran detectives I've known, and she's got a skewed perspective that almost always picks up things other people miss. I'm not trying to tell you your job, Lieutenant, but she's already in the middle of your case, with the people she knows out there. Frankly, she's pretty bullheaded. I'd be willing to bet she's investigating on her own, regardless."

"There are a few ways I could manage to arrest her for that," Donatello said.

Danny sighed. This was not going how he'd hoped. He looked up at Audrey, who was shaking her head, eyebrows raised, as if to say, *What did you expect, kid?*

Suddenly Audrey got up from her desk and walked over to rip the phone from Danny's grip.

"Lieutenant? Detective Audrey Gaines here. Detective Mariano is my partner. I've got to tell you, I don't approve of civilian involvement in an investigation myself. Over here, though, Jenna Blake isn't considered a civilian because she works with the M.E. Maybe you've been following the Jim Kerchak murder case on the news? It's the one your little situation out there has recently eclipsed?"

Danny frowned, not sure where Audrey was going with that.

"We've had a breakthrough on the case, which I can't discuss in any detail right now. While Jenna Blake wasn't responsible for the breakthrough itself, it was her insight which led to the avenue of investigation which allowed for that breakthrough."

For a few seconds Danny glanced around the room

for the real Audrey Gaines. He was stunned to find her coming to Jenna's aid in this way. Not that she didn't like Jenna, but she had never really accepted her as part of the team.

"Great. Thanks for your time," Audrey finished, and hung up Danny's phone. She glared at him. "What are you looking at?"

"An alien body snatcher who stole my partner and took her place."

She gave him the finger and went back to her desk.

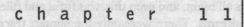

chapter 11

On Tuesday morning, New Year's Eve, Jenna woke up early to make pancakes. April was rushing to get ready to go to the hospital and barely noticed her puttering around the kitchen, dumping Bisquik into a bowl and putting on a pot of coffee. Jenna let the batter sit for a few minutes, and when she heard the blow-dryer whining in the upstairs bathroom, she poured the batter onto the pan in small dollops.

Silver dollar pancakes, with Log Cabin syrup. *The way it's supposed to be,* she thought. When her mother came into the kitchen, Jenna was standing in front of the stove with a spatula in her hand. Her hair was tied back and she wore a faded Wile E. Coyote T-shirt and her mother's ragged old slippers—the linoleum was very cold that morning.

"Wow, isn't this a treat?" April said happily.

"Pancakes served by the living dead," Jenna replied. "Yup. Everyone should try it some time."

"You didn't sleep well?" her mother asked, brow furrowed with concern.

"You could say that."

The truth was, she didn't think she'd slept a total of four hours all night, and even that was fitful and filled with odd dreams. There were only the faintest traces of those dreams left by now, but she knew that John Gage had been in them. And Chris Meserve. They had been whispering something to Jenna. Her parents had been in the room with them, and her father's fiancée, Shayna. Slick had been there, too.

In the dream Jenna had a long knife in her hand.

"Anyway," she said, glancing quickly at the pancakes on the stove. "Time for breakfast."

"And I was going to get a coffee and bagel at Dunkin' Donuts," April told her. "Maybe you should come home more often."

"Don't get carried away, Mom. It's a once-a-year thing at best. Next you'll be wanting me to bring it to you in bed."

"Well . . ." April shrugged as if to say, *That sounds reasonable.*

"Which would require me to be awake before you," Jenna reminded her.

"Ah." April nodded. "Got to keep the reins on my reality here."

"Exactly."

They settled down to eat breakfast. Jenna alternated between coffee and juice, which made her mother cringe. April believed that it was necessary to drink one first, then the other. Jenna had never understood that. Though she checked the clock on the wall a few times during breakfast, April cleared the dishes when they were done. As she was rinsing them in the sink, she glanced over at her daughter.

"How are you doing, Jenna? With all of this, I mean?"

The smile disappeared from Jenna's face. "I'll be okay. I just . . . I want to know what's going on. I'd like to help."

"But nobody will let you."

"Pretty much," Jenna agreed.

As April finished with the dishes, Jenna watched her, letting the feeling of home comfort her. It hadn't been much of a vacation being back in Natick, and it didn't feel much like home, though she'd only been gone a few months. But here, inside these walls, and with her mother, it felt right. *This was what home is about*, she thought.

It was a wistful thought, one that carried her elsewhere, just for a moment, and when she came back from that place, April was looking at her.

"You went to the Bahamas for a minute," her mother said.

Jenna laughed softly. "Then I came back," she agreed, voice tinged with regret.

"I'm worried about you, Jenna. I know this thing is important to you, but you're letting it get far too deep under your skin. You've hardly spent any time with your friends, and—"

"My friends are at Somerset, or they will be when vacation's over," she said, surprising herself with the bitterness in her voice.

"Whoa," April said, eyes widening. "What's that about?"

With a sigh, Jenna shrugged. "I just feel like nobody here knows me anymore, Mom. Except you. To them, I'll always just be the girl with the auburn hair who got all A's and B's and hung out with Moira Kearney."

When her mother didn't reply, Jenna looked up at her curiously. April offered a dubious grin.

"I wish I could say you're wrong, honey. The problem is, I'm not sure you are. If you stay close—I mean, really close—to Moira or Priya, that won't really be true. You guys will start to understand each other as adults, and your relationship will change. But to most of your old friends, well, you're right. You'll always be that girl."

"Thanks, Mom. You've been helpful," Jenna said sarcastically.

April walked over and began to rub Jenna's shoulders, relaxing her, comforting her. As she always did.

"And you'll always be my little girl," she whispered. "But I can't stop you from growing up, and they can't stop you from becoming whatever it is you will become. When you're in school, the same things that are important to you are important to most of the people around you. That makes it easier to be friends. As you get older, your priorities become much more individual."

Jenna chuckled drily. "You can say that again."

April kissed her daughter on the head, then went to the hall closet to grab her winter coat.

"In spite of all that's happened," she said, walking

back in, "you should enjoy them while you're home. Tonight's New Year's Eve. Do *something*, Jenna. I'm sure they just don't know what to make of your motivation. Not many kids your age are as directed as you are. Out of those, I doubt you'll find a single one who does what you do."

"Great." Jenna sighed. "I'm a freak."

"Yup," April confirmed, as she walked toward the door. "And I'm very proud of you for it."

Jenna laughed and mock glared at her mother as she left. After she was gone, Jenna was surprised to find that she actually was feeling better. Her mother had treated her like an adult. She hadn't tried to make the bad news not exist. Instead, she had put it in perspective. Jenna appreciated that in ways she could probably never express. She still couldn't wait to get back to Somerset, but while she was here, there wasn't any reason she shouldn't hang around with her old friends.

Priya in particular. Moira seemed to be getting along just fine, but Jenna thought Priya needed someone to hold her hand, just a little. She didn't mind the thought that she might be that person. In truth, it made her feel good to think that Priya needed her.

Spurred on by that thought, she called Priya and Moira to make plans for that night. As her mother had said, it was New Year's Eve, after all. Both girls had called her the previous day, trying to make plans, and she hadn't bothered to call them back. Neither of them mentioned it, and Jenna was glad.

Jenna had expected Moira to know of a party, and

to want to go. She was right about the first part, but Moira surprised her a little, too.

"I'd just like a girls' night out, y'know? The party thing is so weird. I've had enough of talking about what teachers we hated in high school."

"Totally with you," Jenna vowed.

They decided to have dinner at Uno's and then see a movie. Jenna knew there would be an argument over which movie—there always was—but that was all right. It was just the way it was with them.

"We're getting old," Moira said with a sigh. "What a lame way to spend New Year's Eve."

"Older, not old. And if you'd rather drink till you puke, I won't stop you. But I also won't hold your hair back while you're doubled over to keep you from getting vomit on it. Once was enough."

"You *had* to bring that up."

"It's my duty as your friend to humiliate you," Jenna reminded her.

"Of course," Moira agreed.

When Jenna hung up the phone, she was grinning. Suddenly she felt like things were going to be all right with them. Maybe they thought it was freaky what she was doing. But how could she blame them?

A bit later, as she was getting out of the shower, she heard the phone ring. She quickly wrapped a towel around herself and ran into her mother's room to answer.

"Happy New Year," Damon said.

"You've got about fourteen hours to go, babe."

"I'm not even counting that," he replied. "I've got

eight days till I see you again. That's the only math in my head right now."

"Sweet talker. You're back from Florida?"

"Uh-huh. So what are you up to?"

"Just got out of the shower."

"Just?"

"Get your mind out of the gutter, Mr. Harris," Jenna warned.

"It's my home." Damon sighed. "Really, though, what are you up to?"

"Girls' night. Boring stuff. A movie, probably. What about you?"

"There's a party."

"Where there will be lots of scantily clad girls," Jenna added.

"Girls, yes. As for scantily clad, it's New Jersey, the dead of winter. If scantily clad includes parkas, then yeah. How've things been going with the murder case there? Any developments?"

Jenna hesitated. She didn't want to unload her woes on him. And she didn't really want to dredge them up again, after her mother had just made such an effort to comfort her. On the other hand, she had been bemoaning the fact that she didn't have Damon and Yoshiko and Hunter to bounce things off, other than the occasional e-mail or phone call.

So she told him what she knew. And what she suspected.

"I've been wracking my brain, but I just can't figure out how the three of them are connected besides the fact that they all went to Natick High with me," Jenna explained. "Okay, all the same age, from the same town. But not all male, not all going to the same college or anything. There must be something I'm missing."

"Well, keep going," Damon said thoughtfully. "Work it out. What else do they have in common?"

"Nothing," Jenna said, exasperated.

"Nothing?" Damon asked, dubiously. "Did they ever hang together? Go to summer camp together?"

"Not as far as I've been able to find out."

"Well, are they all white?"

Jenna blinked. "Huh?"

"Not that it's racial or anything. It's a little thing. I mean, do they all have the same eye color, what? This is your line, not mine, but I figure if you start with the smallest things, at least you'll feel like you're getting somewhere."

Jenna thought about that. She wasn't sure it would make her feel any better if she wasn't making any real progress, but she also appreciated that Damon was trying to help.

"They're all white," she agreed. "But they don't have the same hair color or eye color, I don't think. Chris is four or five inches shorter than John. They go to college on different coasts. I don't know. I just . . . it's terrible that this all had to happen at Christmas. It just . . . it's ruined it for everybody I know, but I can't imagine what it'll do for them, and the people really close to them, for the rest of their—"

Jenna stopped speaking abruptly. Her fingers tightened on the phone. Her eyes widened and she stared at nothing.

"Hey. You there?" Damon asked, concern in his voice.

"Oh, God," she whispered in return. "They're all Christian."

Damon didn't get it. "And?"

Mind racing, Jenna ran her fingers through her hair, which was drying in a tangle. She wrapped the towel more tightly around her, thinking.

"Jenna?"

"Christmas, Damon. They all celebrated Christmas. They didn't do this on their own, right? The more I think about it, the more that seems obvious to me. Which means they were either drugged or hypnotized or something. So how could somebody get to all three of them without anybody noticing anything? Maybe whatever they got was in something? A present. Coated with some poison or . . ."

It all fell apart for her. "That doesn't make much sense, does it? I mean, anybody could have touched it. And how could they have specific instructions as to what to do? I'm losing it. Maybe it is all coincidence."

"It isn't any crazier than the cops blaming video games," Damon pointed out.

As Jenna was rolling his words over in her head, the doorbell rang.

"Oh, God, there's someone at the door. Gotta go!"

"Okay, but, Jenna—"

"Talk to you later."

"Jenna!"

"What?"

"Put some clothes on."

Jenna glanced down at the towel wrapped around her as the doorbell rang again. She swore, hung up the phone, and raced to her room.

"Be right there!" she cried.

Moments later, in ragged jeans and a tank top that had been the first thing her hand touched, Jenna opened the door. Vic Grillo and Mike Brody were standing on the front stoop.

"Oh," Jenna said, a bit shocked and self-conscious about her appearance. "Detectives. Hi. Can I help you with something?"

Brody grimaced at that. He looked at his partner and shook his head.

"Miss Blake, we'd like you to come down to the police station with us," Grillo said, his tone grave.

Jenna waited for him to say something else. It wasn't the kind of request she got every day, and it had thrown her. After a moment, she nodded.

"Can you just give me a couple of minutes?" she asked.

Brody turned around and started walking down the path in front of the house.

"We'll wait in the car," Grillo announced, before following Brody.

"Great," Jenna muttered as she closed the door. "This should be fun."

Mark Dufresne—or Special Agent Dufresne, as he preferred to be called—didn't look much like other FBI agents Walter had met. Most of them were just regular folks, but Special Agent Dufresne didn't look like a real FBI agent, he looked like he played one on TV.

"So, in summation," Special Agent Dufresne was saying, "we've got the Marchese woman's deposition. She's picked Guy Bonnano out of a photo spread of known Schiavelli associates as the actual killer. We think we can turn Bonnano. With Dr. Slikowski's testimony, that's damning enough that the FBI is prepared to take Frank Schiavelli into custody."

Walter had been rather silent during the meeting, mainly answering questions posed to him about his deductive reasoning. Now he perked up, disturbed by Special Agent Dufresne's plan of action.

"Excuse me. You're suggesting that the man who actually killed Jim Kerchak, who murdered the mayor with his bare hands, will be asked to turn state's evidence? What will he receive in exchange?"

Special Agent Dufresne didn't like the question. He knew where it was going, and where it was coming from. "I know that you were friendly with the mayor, Dr. Slikowski. But you have to realize that Schiavelli is a much more valuable target. Bonnano's just a grunt. Schiavelli's the real killer, a much more dangerous man. If we can put him away, we can undermine organized crime in Boston for months, and probably keep them on their toes for years to come.

"Bonnano won't serve the time he deserves—nor will Marchese, for that matter—but our real goal is to crucify Schiavelli, and that is as close to a certainty as we ever get in our line of work."

Walter was still far from happy about the arrangement, but he didn't argue. He knew it would be useless. For a moment he tried to think of a suitable response, some kind of tacit protest, but then he glanced at Danny and Audrey, saw the distaste with which they regarded what Special Agent Dufresne had said, and decided to keep silent.

He didn't doubt that the man knew his job. In fact, Audrey had briefed him before the FBI man arrived. Special Agent Dufresne had an excellent reputation, based not only on his record, but also on word of mouth from members of other law enforcement organizations. He was a good man, a talented investigator.

It didn't make Walter feel any better to find out that the man who broke Jim Kerchak's neck was probably headed for witness relocation. Sure, Schiavelli would pay, and he deserved it. But it was only half a victory, and he wasn't looking forward to telling Natalie.

Their meeting ended shortly thereafter, but Special Agent Dufresne lingered, getting himself a second cup of coffee, and the four of them sat around the stained table in the coffee room. Walter wanted to excuse himself, but didn't want to be rude, so he waited for the right opportunity.

He was only half listening as the detectives began to trade bizarre stories with Dufresne. Audrey related the events of a recent case in which a college student had used a toxic powder to temporarily turn several people into zombies. They hadn't died, of course, but had been mentally enslaved by the drug. Walter had been too close to that case, and it would be a long time before he'd find it amusing.

Special Agent Dufresne had a few anecdotes of his own. Audrey's story about mind control had obviously sparked a memory.

"You're gonna love this," he said. "Talk about subliminal messages. There was this professor at MIT who was doing research on brain chemistry. He had this theory that you could alter human behavior by showing someone certain patterns of bright light and color. The really crazy part is he ended up in custody because he was using some kind of video to seduce women, like they'd been drugged or something. When he was arrested, he said it was all research."

Danny and Audrey laughed at the absurdity of the story. Walter shook his head, appalled.

But the story stuck in his head.

When Jenna finally discovered what had brought Grillo and Brody to her house, she was astonished.

"Not that I'm not glad," she said, sitting in the back of their unmarked car. "But I don't understand. I mean, I want to help. I'm just surprised that you'd even give me the time of day."

Grillo seemed about to speak, but Brody, who was behind the wheel, interrupted. "Wasn't our idea," he said gruffly.

"Mike," Grillo warned. Then he turned back to Jenna. "Not that we don't appreciate your attitude, but we're already neck deep in this thing. We've got—"

Jenna clucked her tongue. "I know," she said curtly.

"You've got your lieutenant and the mayor and probably the governor breathing down your necks. It's your case, and the last thing you need is some kid pretending to be a detective sticking her nose in and just generally getting in the way. Never mind that the idea that I—smart-ass college girl—might actually be able to help is unimaginable, and that in the unlikely event it were so, you'd never want any other cops to know you'd actually received help from me."

Grillo blinked, frowned.

"That about sum it up?" Jenna asked. "Because I'm sick of apologizing for who I am, for the job that I do, and for wanting to help."

"Yeah," Brody said from behind the wheel. "That about sums it up." He had a broad grin on his face. "I think maybe we misjudged you, kid."

"Jenna."

"Jenna," Brody corrected himself, still grinning. "Look, somebody put in a good word for you, and Lieutenant Donatello figured it couldn't hurt to let you have a go at talking to the suspects. Their lawyers don't object, so what the hell."

Grillo sighed and shrugged. "This isn't the way things are normally done, Jenna. And it would be bad form, and a bad idea altogether, if you talked to the media about this. Just so long as you understand that."

"I do," she said quickly, realizing she had pushed her luck and not wanting to destroy it completely. "Thanks. I'll . . . I'll help if I can, and if I can't, I swear I'll get out of the way."

Brody chuckled again. "Hell, at least it'll break up the monotony."

Jenna spent nearly two hours at the Natick Police Station. Lieutenant Donatello wasn't there. Grillo made excuses for him, but Brody came right out and told her that the lieutenant wanted to be able to deny that he had known she was involved with the case at all.

It was a haunting couple of hours. One of the detectives was with her at all times, but she wished that someone else were there, someone who knew these people as she did. A little perspective. Much as she had been bemoaning the absence of Yoshiko and Hunter and Damon all along, and frustrated as she was because things would have been so different if the case had happened in Somerset—in Slick's jurisdiction—instead of Natick, she now realized that more than anything, she wanted Moira and Priya there.

The irony was not lost on her.

Alisa Farmer would barely speak to her. She was in restraints, under sedation, and in complete denial. Not only did she claim not to remember murdering her family, she refused to believe that they were dead. But there was something in her red-rimmed eyes and bloodless, ghostly features that told Jenna a different story. Part of Alisa knew the truth, and the rest of her was fighting tooth and nail to keep from discovering it.

Jenna knew right off that Alisa wasn't going to be of any help. She wondered if the girl was even sane anymore.

Chris Meserve seemed to be calmer, but was so withdrawn that Jenna could barely get anything out of him. Nor was she surprised. All three of them were under suicide watch, partially because of Chris. When they'd first explained to him what he had done, as they took him into custody, he'd shattered the glass in his parents' storm door on the way out of the house and attempted to cut his own throat.

He had not exhibited any behavior that would suggest that he might try it again, but that didn't stop the police from keeping him in restraints, and under constant observation, as well.

The police had kept the attempted suicide out of the papers. Jenna was not supposed to know, but it was difficult to pretend otherwise. She found herself sneaking not-so-subtle glances at the bandage on his neck as they spoke. She claimed she had just wanted to see him, to say hello, see if he wanted to talk. Chris was suspicious, though, and she couldn't blame him. They hadn't been that close, and the cops hadn't let anyone else in to see him. He recognized it as strange.

Unlike the others, he remembered at least some of what he had done, though he claimed that what he did recall was hazy, as though he'd only dreamed it. He wept as he spoke those words, and Jenna didn't think she'd get anything out of him. She asked him if he'd noticed anything strange in the time since he'd come home from college for the holidays. Weird smells in the house, strange tastes in his food. Anyone watching him. Things out of place around the house. Anything odd at all.

Nothing. Chris either couldn't remember, or didn't bother trying. He thanked her for coming by, but his eyes were just as haunted as Alisa's, and his voice, when he spoke, was dead.

Outside the room where they had spoken, Jenna had to take a moment. Tears had begun to form in the corners of her eyes. Her lip quivered, and she had to force it to stop, force it all to go away.

Not in front of them, she thought, trying not to let Grillo and Brody see her. She was overwhelmed by the horror of these people, who had not only lost all the people closest to them, but now stood accused of their murders.

Accused, and guilty. But with no memory of having done anything.

It tore Jenna apart thinking about that. An image of her mother came to mind, and she shivered.

John Gage was last. He was a bit more . . . alive than the others. He and Jenna had always been friendly, and he was both surprised and glad to see her. He asked about her and her mother, and all the other people they knew from high school. He asked—with a quick glance at Grillo, who stood behind her—if everyone thought he was guilty.

Jenna told him honestly that she didn't know.

"Do *you* think I did it?" he asked, and she finally saw the depth of the pain in his eyes.

"I don't think you're responsible, no," Jenna said, trying to hide the fact that she'd chosen her words carefully.

John didn't notice or opted not to call her on it. She

asked him the same questions she had asked Chris, and the answers weren't much different. Nor had she really expected them to be. They'd been home for only a few days before their worlds had been torn apart. Just a few days.

For Christmas.

None of them spoke about Christmas. There wasn't any magic in it anymore.

Grillo drove her home. They didn't talk on the way. Her interviews had been a bust, but she was pleased to note that he didn't mention it. That he seemed to have stopped treating her like a kid. There was that, at least.

Still, it ate at her that she hadn't had even the slightest glimmer of an idea. Not a moment of inspiration.

"Thanks," she said idly as she got out of the car.

"Thanks for coming down," Grillo told her. "Happy New Year."

"Oh," Jenna said, surprised. She'd completely forgotten that it was New Year's Eve. She wondered if Chris and John and Alisa knew, and what it meant to them.

"You, too." Jenna shut the door, then headed for her house, enjoying the sight of the wreath on the door, the multicolored lights strung on the bushes out front.

She stopped and stared at the house.

Grillo had started to pull away when she shouted for him to stop. He rolled down the passenger window as she walked back to the car.

"What is it?" he asked.

"Probably nothing," she grumbled. "Just a stray thought. It's kind of a pain in the butt, but maybe you could do something for me?"

Grillo looked put upon, but he nodded. "If I can."

"Ask them each to make a list of what they got for Christmas."

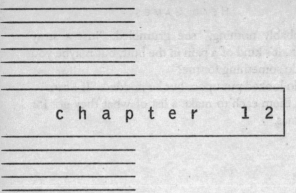

c h a p t e r   1 2

There was a message from Dr. Slikowski on the machine when Jenna got home. When she called him back, neither of them wished the other a happy New Year.

"You called the Natick cops, I guess," Jenna said. "You didn't have to do that, but I appreciate it."

"Actually, I didn't call," he said. "I mentioned your frustration to Danny Mariano. He must have called."

Danny? Jenna thought. Beyond that simple recognition, she wasn't sure what to think. After their brief flirtation, she and Danny had remained friends, certainly. But he'd gone above and beyond with this, vouching for her. Jenna knew she owed him one.

"Still, it was nice of you to take an interest."

"We're a team, Jenna. Or at least, we are when you're not on vacation," Slick assured her.

"Yeah, some vacation."

"I take it the police are allowing you to become more involved?"

She told him about her afternoon. Slick listened carefully, but did not comment while she spoke.

"I only wish the case was in this county," he said. "I would like to be able to be of more help to you."

"You've been helpful already," she told him. "Plus, it isn't like you don't have your own workload. With Dyson away, I'm sure you've had a parade of residents and interns in the autopsy room. And I know how you love that."

Dr. Slikowski chuckled.

"Then there's the mayor's case," Jenna went on.

"Actually, that seems to be drawing to a conclusion," Slick told her. "Which was one of the reasons I wanted to speak with you. The FBI have now gotten involved, as I suspected they might. Things are getting complicated, but they do seem to be heading in the right direction. Schiavelli will end up in prison for his involvement."

There was a momentary silence. Jenna thought Slick was thinking about his friend, the mayor, and the fact that capturing his murderer would do little to bring the man back. She thought that because those were the things in her own mind.

"It's cold comfort, huh?" she said, surprising herself with such a personal question.

Slick paused before responding. Then he uttered a short, dry laugh. "It's justice," he said. "The best any of us can hope for, I suppose."

Jenna grew uncomfortable with the conversation,

and Slick must have, too, for he quickly changed the subject.

"Actually, another reason for my call was that I wanted to share with you something I learned in a meeting with that same FBI agent."

The M.E. went on to relate to Jenna the conversation between the Somerset P.D. detectives and Special Agent Dufresne. She listened intently when he got to the story about the MIT professor.

"I'm not sure I'm following that," she said, though she was fairly certain she was. It was just hard for her to believe. "This professor was experimenting with—"

"The temporary alteration of human brain chemistry resulting in behavioral changes, which are also temporary," Slick explained.

"But to be able to get the desired result, a specific, controlled response, that can't really be possible. It'd be a total shot in the dark," Jenna said, her mind spinning.

"Probably," Slick agreed. "But let's look at it as objectively as we can. You believe that your three former classmates were either all independently exposed to some substance that led to these behavioral changes, or that they were somehow manipulated into doing what they did. If the latter was the case, what form would such manipulation take? When Special Agent Dufresne mentioned this research, it seemed a concept worth repeating to you."

Jenna didn't respond. There was something nagging at the back of her mind. The things that Slick had told her were ringing a bell somewhere, but she couldn't quite put her finger on it. Not yet.

The movie theater at the Natick Mall was a huge, garish thing with all the bells and whistles. If Mardi Gras were a building, this would have been it. Lights and splashes of color and more parking spaces than Disney World, or so it seemed. There were twenty screens, including one dedicated to independent films on a regular basis, and three restaurants inside the theater.

When Jenna was little, there had been two malls, one on either side of the Framingham/Natick border, and two major movie theaters, one of which was attached to a mall. Not this thing. It was off by itself— its own destination—and it was almost always mobbed. In spite of the fact that it was New Year's Eve, or perhaps because of it, the parking lot was jammed.

"This is unbelievable," Jenna muttered, doing her best to maneuver the vehicle through the people and the cars jockeying for a space.

"It's always like this," Priya said.

Jenna glanced at her, saw Priya wince. She had just unintentionally reminded them that she'd been home for a while. It made her uncomfortable, but Jenna decided that maybe it was time to change that.

"Seen a lot of movies lately, Pri?" she asked, grinning. Teasing.

For a second she thought Priya might get angry. There was a flash in her dark eyes that said she wasn't quite sure if Jenna's words were lighthearted and loving or meant to cut. Then she softened, relaxed.

"Too many," Priya said. "I haven't had much else to do with myself."

In the backseat, Moira sort of grunted. "I don't know why you didn't think you could tell us, Priya. All that time you could've been visiting Jenna at school, meeting some Somerset guys. You could've flown out and hung with me and gotten an idea what California boys are like."

Suddenly Moira leaned forward, hands on the front seat, straining against her seat belt. "Hey, that's an idea. You should come out this semester. I mean, you're not going to start back to school till fall, right? You should come visit me. It'd be great."

Jenna was slowly, patiently navigating through the lot, following people who were coming out of the theater, hoping that she might be able to snag their parking spot before someone else did. But though her attention was on her driving, she managed to notice how Priya brightened.

"Really?" Priya asked. "That'd be cool, Moira. Thanks." She looked at Jenna. "We should all go! Maybe for spring break or something? What do you think, Jenna? Talk about a party."

Jenna smiled. It was the first time she had seen Priya that enthused, that unguarded, since she'd come home for the holidays. The last thing she wanted to do was to take that enthusiasm away from her. So, instead of giving an honest response—that she'd already planned to hang with her college friends for spring break—she only nodded.

"Yeah, maybe," she said. "Sounds cool."

With a glance in the rearview mirror, Jenna saw that Moira had caught her tone, and her lack of interest in the idea. Moira raised an eyebrow, just slightly, and glanced out the window.

Up ahead, a thirtysomething couple was sliding into their Jeep Grand Cherokee, and Jenna clicked on her turn signal to let other cars know that she had claimed their spot. A Volkswagen zoomed around her, its driver likely just as frustrated as she had been until she'd found the space.

Priya and Moira talked a little about the potential trip. Jenna remained silent. After a moment, though, Priya seemed to hesitate. She glanced from Jenna to Moira and then back.

"You guys, I just want to say thanks for this."

"For what?" Jenna asked.

"Just this. Hanging out. Taking the time. Being my friends. I don't know what I'd do without you guys. I know you must think I'm a wicked loser, but—"

"Priya!" Moira said curtly.

Jenna put the car in Park and looked over at Priya. "You know that isn't true. You tried a new thing, it didn't work out, and now you're moving on. That's the way life works, I think. I mean, I bailed on this job with Dr. Slikowski, but after I had some time to regroup, I went back to it. We're young enough to take chances and make mistakes."

She looked back at Moira, who appeared a little

doubtful of Jenna's words, then spoke to Priya. "No matter what happens in life, no matter where we all end up or what we end up doing, we'll always be your friends. Right, Moira?"

Moira blinked, surprised that Jenna had turned the conversation to her.

"Absolutely," Moira confirmed.

A sheepish grin spread across Priya's face. "Thanks, guys."

There was a moment then. Something they all shared in. It was a millisecond of love and loyalty that made Jenna feel, for just a moment, that she had stepped back through time nearly one whole year. Perhaps more. All the misgivings she'd had about coming home, and the way everyone expected time to just freeze and nobody to ever be any different . . . all of those feelings just went away.

Dr. Slikowski's comments earlier, and the story told to him by the FBI agent whose name she could not remember, had lingered in her mind. It grew more and more solid and significant in her head until she became determined to pursue that line of investigation first thing in the morning.

But that was then, and this was now. New Year's Eve. Girls' night out. As they got out of the car, their talk turned to silly things. Christmas presents and the dread of college classes resuming and some of the teachers they'd had in high school. Soon, they were giggling together, mostly about Noah.

It seemed that one of the reasons none of them had wanted Noah to come along that night was because they wanted to talk about him. Neither Priya nor Moira had any interest in going out with Noah again, much as they loved him. He was a guy, and eighteen years old, and as far as the three of them were concerned, that meant he pretty much had no control whatsoever over his thoughts, words, or actions.

"He doesn't even know it," Moira said, chuckling. "That's the funny thing. Noah's like the nicest guy I know, and it's not about flirting or seduction or anything. But if you said, 'Hey, Noah, wanna go fool around?' he'd be there in a heartbeat."

"Have gun, will travel," Jenna said.

The three of them laughed as they walked toward the front of the theater. Priya glanced at Jenna.

"Where the hell does that saying come from, anyway? You always used to say that about guys. I'm pretty sure I know what *you* mean by it, but what does it *really* mean?"

Moira nodded in agreement. She didn't know the origin of the phrase either, though they'd used it frequently enough in school to talk about how endlessly driven by sex guys were.

"It's an old TV show," Jenna told them. "A western, I think. I remember my mother talking about it when I was really little. It was my father's favorite show or something. Maybe my mom used it to mean the same thing." She smiled at the thought. "The guy was a hired gunfighter, or something. His slogan was 'Have gun, will travel,' like he'd go anywhere to do a job."

Moira held the door as they went in. People were

packed inside, lined up as if the next *Star Wars* movie was about to open or something.

"That should be your slogan, too," Moira said a bit sarcastically.

Jenna frowned, not understanding. "Huh?"

"Have scalpel, will travel." Moira grinned. "Jenna Blake, the dead man's Nancy Drew."

A hot jolt of anger flashed through Jenna. Her jaw clenched, and she glanced at Priya, who looked away. *At least she has the good sense to be uncomfortable*, Jenna thought.

Then she looked at Moira.

"Go to hell."

All the good feeling she'd had just moments earlier was suddenly burned away. Moira didn't even seem shocked by her reaction; it was almost as though she'd expected it. And didn't mind.

"Come on, Jenna. I'm just teasing. I just think you get a little carried away with the whole *Murder, She Wrote* thing. I know that you've worked with Dr. Spandowski—"

"Slikowski."

"Whatever," Moira said, exasperated. "It's a cool job. Very grown-up. You've always been a little more grown-up than the rest of us, and I've always admired you for it. But just because Dr. Whatever helps the police with murder investigations, that doesn't make him Batman, and it sure as hell doesn't make you Robin."

It took Jenna a moment to realize how foolish she must look. Her mouth was open slightly, though she hadn't been aware of it happening. Her eyes were wide, her expression pained. Moira looked unsure of herself, but nowhere near as much as Jenna thought she ought to.

"You don't know what you're talking about," Jenna told her. "Maybe you should stop now. Talking, I mean."

Moira blinked. "Jenna, I'm not . . . look, I just mean—"

"You mean I'm just a kid getting carried away with some kind of fantasy world where I help the police solve crimes," she snapped loudly.

Several people turned to look at them in line, and at least one couple were leaning in, actively listening to the conversation. Jenna lowered her voice.

"I've tried to explain this to you," she said angrily, though her voice was barely above a whisper. "I'll do it one more time. I have contributed to the solution of several murder investigations in the past few months. I am not a cop. I'm not a detective. I'm not even a criminologist. But I do work for the medical examiner, and I do look into pathology and forensic issues, helping the police.

"Obviously that makes you uncomfortable for some reason. But let me tell you this much, you can drag out all the insults and stupid pop-culture references you want, and it won't change the fact that I have done these things. I don't get you, Moira. Is it that you still want to be in high school, that you've got some kind of never-grow-up Peter Pan thing going on? 'Cause I can tell you—for my part—I'm done with high school."

Moira looked as though she regretted opening her mouth. But somehow, in a way Jenna couldn't really explain, she didn't exactly look sorry. Maybe it was something in her eyes, but Jenna didn't think Moira cared about the conversation they were having, except that it was embarrassing to be having even a whispered argument in front of a bunch of people waiting to see a movie.

"Guys, come on," Priya said in hushed tones. "Jenna, you know she didn't mean anything by it. This is *us* here. Come on. Moira, give Jenna some credit. And you, Jenna, give her a break. We're all reeling from this thing, and I guess when you talk about these things like you might be able to do something about them, it makes us all feel a little stupid and useless."

Jenna blinked. She looked at Moira and saw that there was a little bit of truth in what Priya had said.

"So what, then?" she demanded, glaring at them both. "I'm not supposed to try to help? If I think I can do something, I should just keep quiet about it so it doesn't make you guys feel weird?"

"That's not what I'm saying," Priya quickly retorted.

"Then what *are* you saying?" Jenna asked.

Moira moved in close, and put a hand on Jenna's arm. "What she's saying, Blake, is that when you go talking to the families of people in trouble, like you talked to Todd Gage, you're doing one of two things: coming off like some psycho or offering false hope."

"Ah," Jenna sighed. It all became clear to her. Todd Gage had been telling people about their talk, and

Moira was embarrassed. Probably Priya was embarrassed, too.

She shook her head. "Look, if you guys are humiliated by what other people may say about me, then maybe you should put a little distance between us. If I think I can help, I'm not going to do nothing just so you won't feel like people who are laughing at me are laughing at you, too."

They both began to respond, but then, to everyone's surprise, it was suddenly their turn to buy tickets. Jenna wanted to turn around and walk out of there. The thought of spending two more hours with her friends did not appeal to her in the least. But if she did that, she knew that they would have to call someone for a ride home, and it would drive even more of a wedge between them.

Instead of bolting, she bought her ticket for Antonio Banderas's latest film. Behind the counter, she saw a little sign discussing a midnight showing of *The Matrix*, and she suddenly understood the lines. Sure, it was available on video, but midnight showings of the film had become quite popular. It was a huge commercial success, but it was also a cult classic, the kind of thing people liked to see in the movie theaters over and over.

The conversation came to a dead stop right there. They bought popcorn and sodas, and Priya got a big bag of Twizzlers that she would probably share, and the three of them went in to watch the movie. Priya sat between them, as if Jenna and Moira were squabbling children. All through the film, Jenna stewed.

When it was over, Priya and Moira talked about the movie, giving it their usual play-by-play review, with special attention paid to Antonio's butt. Jenna participated mainly in grunts and gestures. It wasn't until they were out in the lot again, standing around waiting to get into her car, that she spoke up.

"Earlier today I met with the detectives from Natick Homicide who are working these cases. They asked me to talk to Alisa and Chris and John, and I did. There's no doubt in my mind that they did the things they're accused of. But I think someone engineered it. Someone found a way to toy with their minds to make them do this. I'm supposed to meet with the cops again tomorrow morning, to give them whatever feedback I have.

"I'm not going to say I know how it was done. But I think I've come up with a way that it *could* have been done. A way John and the others could have been made to do what they did. In some ways, it's a crazy tangent. But in other ways, it makes so much more sense than any of the options they've come up with so far. If I'm right, then either I'll find out who did it, or the police will, using information I provide to them."

Priya and Moira stared at her.

"So?" Priya asked. "Let's have it."

Jenna hesitated.

"We won't say anything, Jenna," Priya went on. "Even if you guys are pissed at each other, you've got to know that."

With a sigh, Jenna nodded. "Remember a couple of

years ago, when all those kids in Japan had seizures while watching that cartoon?"

Both girls nodded, vague expressions on their faces. She understood. When Slick had brought up the cartoon connection, she had no idea where he might be going with it. But once he explained, it made a sick sort of sense. To him, it was little more than a kind of intuition. In her mind, however, it had all truly begun to come together.

"I think someone's turned that into a science. See, in that situation, the combination of light and colors and maybe even sounds caused a chemical reaction in the brains of those kids, and caused those seizures. There's an MIT professor who's been doing research on just that subject. I think somebody, maybe even that professor, found the perfect visual formula to cause someone to go into a kind of homicidal trance, and put it on a videotape. I think that same person sent those videos to Chris and John and Alisa, maybe as Christmas presents."

Jenna paused, watched their reactions. "It'd be the perfect weapon, wouldn't it? You could make the most peaceful person into your own monster, just for a little while. Anytime, anywhere. All the nasty little covert operations groups would just love that."

Finally Moira whispered, "You're serious?"

"Of course I'm serious," Jenna snapped. "God, Moira, don't you get it? I've been serious all along. Whatever you may think of me, I'd think you would have known that from the start. This has never been a game for me, it isn't some lark like taking Russian lessons for two days and dropping out. This is all very real, though God knows I wish it weren't. So make all the jokes you want about Nancy Drew or Jessica Fletcher, but keep them to yourself.

"This isn't fun for me, and it isn't a game."

Jenna climbed into the car and started it up. Priya and Moira belted themselves in.

"I . . . Jenna, I never meant . . ." Moira began weakly. Then her voice trailed off, and she didn't break the silence again except to say good night when Jenna dropped her off.

"You really think you know what happened in all this?" Priya asked a short time later, as Jenna pulled in front of her house.

"I think I do," Jenna said.

"I hope you're right," Priya replied softly. "I really hope so."

Jenna turned to look at her, saw the love in Priya's eyes.

"Hey, Pri, I'm sorry about all that. I know we ruined your night."

"No." Priya shook her head. "It was fine. A real experience. Just do me one favor?"

Tilting her head to one side, Jenna arched an eyebrow curiously.

"Keep me posted. If you're right about this, and somebody made all of this happen . . . I hope it's over."

Jenna couldn't have agreed more. The entire drive home, she tried not to be mad at Moira, tried to make excuses for her attitude. It wasn't entirely successful.

Which only added to her surprise when she walked in the front door to find her mother on the phone with Moira, who had just called. April smiled and handed her the phone, then poured herself a glass of milk and went to sit down in front of the TV. Clearly, she had waited up for Jenna so that they could share the New Year together.

"What's up?" Jenna asked, her tone neutral.

"I was thinking about what you said," Moira told her. "It's been a few days, or it would have come to me sooner. But I realized as you were driving away . . . I think I got one of those videos for Christmas."

Jenna felt all the air rush from her lungs. In the other room, her mother was calling for her. She could hear a crowd counting down, people shouting and cheering.

"Jenna?" Moira asked, on the other line. "What should I do?"

The countdown reached "one." April came into the kitchen, grinning, and blew a horn at Jenna. Then she saw the expression on her daughter's face, and all the boisterousness left her.

"Jenna?" Moira said again.

Jenna's voice shook. "Happy New Year."

chapter 13

New Year's Day. To Jenna it seemed that most of the time, all of America becomes a ghost town. Nobody on the streets. Nobody on the highways. Like the hotel in *The Shining*, or the whole world in *Omega Man*, Natick was deserted on New Year's Day. People tended to stay in and nurse their hangovers, or just watch television, maybe do some chores around the house.

More than any other, it was a day of rest.

Not this year, she thought grimly.

The new year began with a flurry of activity. Jenna called Detective Grillo first thing in the morning. Though he and Brody had no love for her—were, more than likely, leaning toward the sardonic and dismissive in her regard—the cops took her seriously enough to act almost instantly on her tip. The city of Natick was turned upside down, all throughout that long, loneliest of winter days.

By the time Jenna met with them again, in the homicide squad room at the Natick Police Department, the records of the previous year's Natick High graduating class had been pored over as though they held some great theological significance. Parents and former students were pressed for information.

At the meeting Jenna was not at all surprised to see that the FBI had sent an agent down—Special Agent Mark Dufresne, to be precise. Grillo and Brody were there, as was Lieutenant Donatello, who frowned at her, though she knew it had to have been his idea for her to be there. She didn't think the lieutenant liked the idea of having a kid around, no matter how much help she might be.

"All right," Dufresne said, taking the lead, "what've we got?"

He looked at Donatello, but the lieutenant gestured toward his detectives, and it was Grillo who sat up straight, adjusted his glasses, and glanced at the notes on the table in front of him.

"At this point, it appears that at least twenty-two of Miss Blake's former classmates received the videotape. Most of them have watched it already without any adverse affects. But we haven't done all of the interviews. We're still tracking down some of the potential recipients. Obviously, our first priority has been to make sure this doesn't happen again."

Brody grunted. "I'm still not sure I believe any of this. Just by flashing some bright lights in someone's face, you can turn 'em into a killer like flipping a switch?"

Special Agent Dufresne cleared his throat. He looked cautiously at Jenna before addressing the cops. "Believe it," he said.

"You have to admit, it's incredible," Lieutenant Donatello said.

"Think about the numbers, and it's easier to believe," Jenna pointed out. "I mean, three out of at least twenty-two, maybe more. That's not great odds. It worked on three people, but it didn't work on any of the others."

Brody looked thoughtful, but Dufresne skirted Jenna's comment. "What about the tapes? We got anything there?"

"According to the kids we interviewed," Grillo replied, glancing at Jenna on the word *kids*, "it was literally only flashes of light and swirls of color. I'm surprised *Fantasia* never sent anybody into a murderous rage, if that's all it takes. Anyway, all but three of them had thrown the tapes away after looking at them. The three we got our hands on are all blank."

"Self-erasing," Dufresne muttered. "This guy is smart."

"I'm not all that broken up about it," Brody chimed in, trying to tuck his shirt in and failing. "If watching this thing makes people go nuts, I'd rather we all pass. Especially those of us with guns."

Lieutenant Donatello was nodding slowly. Then he looked at Dufresne. "Do you have any leads on that professor. The guy at MIT?"

"Franz Schechter," Dufresne replied. "He was dismissed two months ago. We're having a little trouble tracking him down. But give it a day or so. Anyway, I don't think it's Schechter."

Jenna noticed the frown on Lieutenant Donatello's face. Grillo and Brody both seemed a bit surprised as well.

"We can't just discount him. He's already been in trouble once for abusing this kind of science," Grillo pointed out.

"No, you're right," Jenna said quickly. "But where's the connection? I mean, why Natick? Why these particular kids? My class? Whoever did this is brilliant, no question. But if we're looking for a link, we should check the class registration for Schechter's courses the last couple of years, see if there are any students from Natick High."

Dufresne smiled at her. "Very good, Miss Blake. That's exactly what the Bureau is doing right now."

Brody scoffed. "A student? You think some teenager is behind this? Come on. This is mad scientist stuff. The mind that came up with this thing . . ."

His words trailed off as he noticed Jenna, saw the frustration on her face. Brody shook his head and chuckled.

"Then again," he said.

"Yes, then again," Dufresne said. "While we're tracking Schechter, and he's most certainly a suspect, our profiling team is looking at brilliant young people, eighteen to twenty, probably but not necessarily Christian, who graduated from Natick High in the last three years."

Lieutenant Donatello nodded. "He *could* be Christian. Planting the tapes to be opened as Christmas gifts was pretty convenient, and might indicate that he's most familiar with Christmas customs rather than another holiday. But he could just as easily be anti-Christian, choosing his subjects that way. There's no way to know."

"True," Dufresne agreed. "Also, I wanted to mention that I'm having an agent do up a report of similar cases, anything at all, that we can all go over. It's important we understand the science here, if possible."

A small chuckle escaped Jenna's lips.

"Miss Blake?" Special Agent Dufresne asked.

"Just remembering that you all wanted to blame video game violence," she said. "And here we have videotapes instead. Only this time, nobody can say it was the movie or TV show that did it, it was a person. A person behind it all."

"True," Grillo agreed. "But what set this person off? And let's face it, you've just finished explaining that you think it's someone your age."

"Oh, but people over the age of twenty never crack and go loony and start blowing people away," Jenna sneered. "I'm so sick of this supposition that younger people can't distinguish reality from fantasy. That's only true if you've grown up in a home where that separation is never made. Sometimes our society creates monsters, Detective. That's a fact, sad but true. The age of the monster has no bearing on what it is. And it isn't watching *The Three Stooges* or *The Matrix* that does it. It's the environment in which those things are watched."

"Miss Blake—" Donatello began, his very tone a reminder to Jenna that, unlike when she was with Slick and Danny and Audrey, here she was not among friends.

She found she didn't care.

"Not to mention that a lot of human monsters are just born that way. Simply biology. Take a look at this case, gentlemen. Brain chemistry. Like clinical depression and so many other things. It's so convenient to point to something and say, 'Ooh, that's bad, take it away before these kids get the wrong idea,' instead of taking away the people. And that's exactly what it is—the people who have put out that wrong idea to begin with."

Jenna found that she was breathing a bit heavily, that they were all staring at her. She felt embarrassed. Brody was grinning slightly, but not in a derogatory way. She thought maybe the big detective had come to like her.

"And I guess I'm down off my soapbox now," she said sheepishly.

"All right then," Dufresne went on as if she'd never spoken a word. "I guess we just keep on our current investigative tracks, coordinate information, and create a suspect list. I suggest we start reinterviewing any member of the class in question who did not get one of these tapes at Christmas."

The meeting began to break up. Jenna felt horribly awkward as they all rose and meandered out of the room. She was surprised to find Brody next to her as she walked toward the door.

"I misjudged you, Jenna. You're a kid. I let that put you in a kind of box in my head. As a detective, I should know better than that. Sorry," Brody mumbled.

Jenna brightened. "Not at all, Detective. Thanks for even taking the time to talk to me, and especially for keeping me in the loop."

The detective gave a low, sarcastic laugh. "Keeping *you* in the loop? Kid, if you weren't keeping *us* in the loop, we wouldn't have gotten as far as we have on this case."

After a stammered reply, Jenna went out to her car. Inside, she only sat for a few minutes, smiling softly. Brody had seemed like such a cranky man at first. But his words meant a great deal to her.

He and the others would get to the bottom of things quickly now. The FBI and the Natick police, working together, shouldn't have any trouble figuring out who had engineered all of this tragedy.

It was only a matter of time.

Jenna missed Damon something fierce, not to mention Hunter and Yoshiko. But she also missed school. Somerset University was home for her now, and she felt as though she'd been away too long. Less than a week and she'd be back there full-time. She was surprised at the depth of her anticipation.

For the time that remained to her, she had every intention of enjoying the company of her high school friends, and vowed to herself to hang out with her mother a little more before going back. But for the moment, she wanted to start the new year off just right. So that afternoon, when she got home, she sent Yoshiko a lengthy e-mail, giving her an up-to-the-minute update. Then she called Hunter and was happy to find him home. She'd meant to call him on Christmas, had all but promised Yoshiko she would, and felt guilty that it had taken her this long. Though she did have a good excuse; life had presented plenty of distractions recently.

Hunter's relationship with his mother had improved; she had stopped drinking and had started seeing a therapist for depression. It was better than Jenna had expected. Still, of all of them, she thought Hunter would be the most relieved when classes started up again. Jenna called Damon, too, and they made plans to take her mother out to dinner on Sunday when he got back from Jersey.

It felt good and right.

But there was something more.

After days of depression and sadness and self-doubt, Jenna was feeling pretty good about herself. Though she had needed Dr. Slikowski's help, and would have given anything for him to have been involved with the case, she had managed to get the courtesy and consideration she had been looking for from both the local authorities and the FBI. Plus, she had contributed to the investigation significantly.

It was nice. It was exactly what she needed. But there was more to it. Her small victory had gotten her mind racing, thinking of the autopsies she'd helped with in previous months. She wanted—needed—to get back to that. The job was a thrill, the end result leaving her feeling as though she had truly accomplished something.

All of which made her think of Dr. Slikowski, and the fact that Dyson was still on vacation. She knew he would be quite frustrated working with new people all the time, and it occurred to her that while she was still on vacation, Somerset was only forty minutes away, and there was no reason she couldn't help out if he needed her.

A little after eight o'clock, she spoke to him on the phone, though only briefly. Jenna heard a woman's voice in the background.

"I'm sorry," she said. "Am I interrupting something?"

"I do have a guest," he confirmed. "Natalie Kerchak. An old friend. But I always have a moment to spare for you, Jenna."

He inquired about the "video murders," as he obviously now thought of them, and she filled him in before mentioning that she'd be willing to come in the next day if he needed her.

"Well," Slick replied evasively, "I wouldn't want to trouble you."

"It's no trouble," she insisted.

"Excellent," the M.E. said happily. "How early can you be here?"

Which was how she ended up driving out Route 128 to Route 2 and then up 16 into Somerset the next morning, a huge cup of Dunkin' Donuts coffee on the seat between her legs. New Year's Eve revelry had led to its usual share of tragedy, and there were three autopsies to be done that day. Two of them had been driving drunk, and the third had been struck by a drunk driver on an overpass and knocked over the side, only to plummet to the highway that passed nearly one hundred feet below.

They did that one last. It was the one that tempted her to regret having come in to help. After all, these were not mysterious deaths. The cases were open and shut. The only thing that kept her from regretting her decision to go in and help was how grateful Slick seemed to be that she bothered.

"I really do appreciate your coming in," he told her as they were washing up, once all the work had been completed.

"We're a team," she said happily. "You and me and Dyson, even though he's MIA. If it weren't for you, I might not have figured out the key to the murders in Natick."

Slick nodded in agreement. "And if it weren't for you, I might never have had the breakthrough that led to Frank Schiavelli's arrest. I thank you for that, and Natalie does, too."

Natalie, Jenna thought. Slick seemed to smile just slightly when he said her name. She glanced at him curiously.

"So, this Natalie?" she asked. "The mayor was her brother, you said, right? She's an old friend?"

"That's right," Slick replied.

There was something in his tone that told her that Natalie Kerchak could not be described so simply, not by a long shot.

"Good for you," she said, and then flushed. She hadn't meant it to sound so suggestive.

Slick's expression grew serious. "Maybe," he said. "We'll just have to wait and see about that."

It had grown quite cold that day. As Jenna left Somerset Medical Center a little after five o'clock, it began to snow. She had planned to have dinner with her mother—April was going to make her famous turkey-and-cornflake meatloaf, which was not only the only meatloaf Jenna liked, but it was perfect food for a night like this—but now she realized that she would be home much later than she had planned. Between the rush hour traffic and the snow, she found herself a long way from home.

The road was cold enough that the snow began to pile up quickly. Her headlights cut through the white, but not far. After forty-five minutes, she was still on Route 128, a couple of miles from the Turnpike, and she decided to get off at the next exit and call home. She shivered, standing at a Bell Atlantic kiosk at a Mobil station, and waited while the phone rang four times.

The answering machine picked up. It was a custom-made message, just for her.

"Hi there, you've reached the Blake residence. Jenna, if it's you, I hope you get home safe. I'm going to end up here a lot later than I thought, so you're on your own. I'm sorry. Anyone else, leave a message."

She hung up halfway through the beep, dejected. Her game plan had been to work for Slick and still manage to take advantage of the fact that she was living at home for at least a few more days, hang with Mom, all that. *So much for that,* she thought. *And no meatloaf.* Through her shoes, covered in snow, her toes began to go numb.

Jenna hustled back to the car and was about to pull out when she saw the Burger King sign glowing right next door. Though she hated to eat fast food if she could avoid it, the idea of cooking now appealed to her even less. Reluctantly, she went to the drive-through and ordered dinner.

At least it was hot.

Back on the highway, she punched buttons on the radio and found one station playing "then and now" Santana. As carefully as she could manage, she watched the traffic, held on to the wheel, and ate her food. The whole process was giving her a headache.

By the time she pulled into her mother's driveway half an hour later, Jenna was in a foul mood. The snow had continued to fall, growing heavier and heavier. Plows had already been down the street at least once, and there was an eight-inch wall of snow and ice at the end of the driveway. She crunched over it without a problem, but it was just another minor annoyance among many in the previous couple of hours.

Now, though, it was almost over. The relief was not upon her yet, but she could taste it. Inside her mother's house, the lights were burning warmly, waiting for her. There would be snacks and television or a book. Jenna might even build a fire. Her mom would enjoy that when she got home. A long night of lazing around would do her a world of good.

There was Nesquik in the kitchen cabinet, and it almost called out to her to help it fulfill its true destiny as hot chocolate.

Jenna stepped out of the car, slipped her keys into her pocket, and pulled her jacket more closely around her.

Behind her, blue lights flashed suddenly. Startled, Jenna turned around quickly, slipped on the snowy driveway, and would have gone down hard on her butt if she hadn't grabbed hold of the open door.

The blue light came from a dashboard globe inside an unmarked police car. The dome light inside the car was on, and the passenger door was open. A burly figure sat behind the wheel, face shrouded in darkness.

Brody, she thought.

Which meant the guy walking toward her across the snow-covered lawn had to be Grillo. Jenna shut the door to her car and shoved her hands in her pockets, trying to keep them warm. Waiting.

As Grillo approached, Jenna squinted her eyes to see his face through the falling snow.

His expression was grave.

Elsewhere, he sat in the dark and watched the video monitor in front of him. The room was filled with television screens and VCRs and cable boxes and all manner of recording equipment, both audio and video.

The image on the screen was dark and vague, almost impossible to make out if he didn't know what he was looking at. The night before, when he'd mounted the camera on the tree across the street from the Blake house, the local weathermen hadn't made a peep about any coming storm. *Typical New England,* he thought in frustration.

"Goddamned storm," he muttered.

He moved closer to the monitor, watching as Detective Grillo approached Jenna Blake.

The cavalry, coming to the rescue, he thought, and snickered.

His name is John DeAngelis. Ring a bell?" Detective Grillo watched Jenna's face expectantly.

When he said the name, she blinked in surprise. "Johnny D.?" she said, scoffing. "Come on. No way."

It wasn't her usual response when dealing with law enforcement, but she couldn't help it. The moment Grillo spoke that name, a picture popped into her head. She and Johnny D. had never been friends, but she had known him since she was in the first grade. Johnny had been one year ahead of her all through school. He'd always been a sweet, quiet guy. A loner, but not psychotically so. He never dressed weird, or seemed to have any bizarre obsessions that she could see. Just a nice, clean-cut guy.

"He was the valedictorian of his class," Grillo reminded her. "But grades aren't everything. He was more brilliant than any of the teachers ever knew."

"So he's smart," Jenna argued, defending him. "And

okay, it isn't like I knew him that well. I don't think I ever had one real conversation with him my whole life. But that doesn't mean it was him."

Even as she said it, though, she began to doubt herself. Johnny D. had been part of the scenery of her life for a long time. Wallpaper, maybe a painting on the wall, but certainly no more than that. He was always there, so much so that she rarely if ever noticed him.

He was, if nothing else, very familiar to her.

But that didn't mean he was innocent. It didn't mean he was a good guy. With the snow falling all around, filling the cone of light coming down from a street lamp, covering her hair in a white shroud, Jenna thought of Johnny D. and shivered.

Grillo gave her a sympathetic glance. "There's a lot more to this guy than you know, Jenna. He's been writing to the CIA and other covert agencies for more than three years. That's what he wants to do when he gets out of college. But he's also been making all kinds of crazy promises to them. He's made a lot of comments about experiments he's done, and technology that he can bring to them if they'll hire him."

Jenna stared at him. "Johnny D.? This is Johnny DeAngelis?"

With a nod, Grillo brushed the snow off his shoulders, then wiped his face with his hand. "The FBI tried DeAngelis's dorm room at MIT, and his parents' house here in Natick. No luck. He must have some kind of hideaway, maybe at a relative's or a friend's. They'll find him soon."

She could tell by his hesitation there was more.

"What?" she demanded.

Grillo stood up a little straighter, and met her inquiry with a steady gaze. "We found some things in the kid's room at his parents' house. Newspaper clippings on this case and photographs of nearly everyone involved. He's been following us, watching us try to solve it. Must have been some kind of game to him."

Jenna sighed. "And some of the pictures were of me?"

"You were the only civilian," Grillo confirmed. "That doesn't necessarily mean anything, but just in case, we've got a regular patrol car coming down to keep an eye on the house. Brody and I will be out front until they get here.

"You're staying in the rest of the night?" he asked.

Mutely, Jenna nodded.

"You want me to go into the house with you?"

She shook her head, then looked up at him. "No. I'm . . . I'll be okay."

Grillo stood and watched as Jenna trudged up to her front door. *Johnny D.*, she thought in amazement. There were a couple of people she went to high school with who were not only almost as smart as Johnny was, but who were angry, disenfranchised teenagers, too. Traci Rogers and Steve Banks came immediately to mind. Both were just as likely to give you the finger as say hello in the hall. Both had been arrested at least once for assault; Banks for theft as well. They hated everyone. At least, when they were in high school. In fact, the two of them would have been first on her list if either had gone to MIT.

But Johnny D.?

"Damn," she whispered as she unlocked the door and went inside, shaking the snow from her hair.

Jenna had always had a picture of Johnny D. in her head, an image of him that she admired, though she'd never known him well. She found herself surprised at the level of disappointment she felt to know what he really was.

Inside, she double-locked the door, then took off her boots and her jacket. Upstairs, she found a message on the machine from her mother, checking in and letting her know she hoped to be home by ten o'clock.

It was barely seven. Jenna wished her mother were there, and she would have called to check on her, but if April was still at work, chances were she wasn't exactly able to come to the phone. When April worked a double shift, Jenna knew that she rarely had time for coffee, never mind anything but the most urgent of phone calls.

She made some hot chocolate, then sat down in the living room in front of the television. Her mind was racing, and she wanted to calm it. Half of her wanted to grab a video, something she loved, maybe *Butch Cassidy and the Sundance Kid*, but she didn't think she could concentrate that much. The book she'd just started, *A Cool Breeze on the Underground*, by a writer named Don Winslow, sat unread on the nightstand in her bedroom.

Nope. Tonight, channel surfing was just what the doctor ordered.

She flipped past a couple of old black-and-white movies, reruns of *Drew Carey* and *Friends*, something cheesy but cool on the Sci-Fi Channel, and then settled on *Jeopardy!* Despite her preoccupation, she was able to answer about half the questions before the contestants. The Final Jeopardy category was the Crusades.

The show went to commercial.

Then the cable went out.

Jenna swore under her breath. *Every time there's a big storm,* she thought crankily. Though, as she looked out the window, she had to admit that in spite of the snow the storm wasn't that serious. Resigned to life without cable, she took a couple of sips of her hot chocolate and got up to look in the video cabinet for something to watch. Her fingers danced over the spines of the tapes and stopped on *Say Anything,* with John Cusack. It had been one of her favorites since about the seventh grade. Very romantic.

Which made her think of Damon. Such thoughts, in turn, made her impatient for school to start. She missed him.

Jenna took the videotape, slid it out of the box, and walked over to the entertainment center in the living room. The hiss of the snowy static on the television was loud enough to be annoying, and she turned it down before even turning on the VCR. She was about to slide the tape in when the hissing stopped, the snow disappeared, and a band of color appeared on screen. It appeared that her cable was working again. Sort of.

Words ran across the screen. *We're sorry. Your local*

cable provider is experiencing an interruption in service. Please stand by. Service will return to normal momentarily.

Jenna switched channels. It was on every one.

"That's new," she said.

The bar with the words scrolling across it disappeared, leaving only a weird kind of test pattern in the background. Jenna debated putting in *Say Anything* instead of waiting, but thought she'd give it another half a minute. She watched the television.

A burst of white light filled the screen. Jenna blinked.

"What the hell?" The colors had returned.

Then there came another flash of light.

And she knew.

"Oh God," she whispered, dropping the video. "No way." She punched the eject button on the VCR. One of her mother's exercise tapes popped out. The screen remained the same. She reached out and clicked it off, but it came back on again almost instantly. Without her having touched a button.

Jenna shielded her eyes, thoughts racing. *Gotta find a phone.*

"Hello, Jenna."

Against her will, she looked up at the television screen. The pattern was gone. The lights and swirls gone. There before her was the face of Johnny DeAngelis. He looked tired, haggard, and he needed a shave. The light was bad, but it was most definitely him. The picture quality wasn't great either. It was as though he'd set up a camera in some basement somewhere . . .

That's exactly what he's done, she thought. *It's like somebody's Webcam or something.* But this wasn't a computer. It was the television in her living room.

"Not bad, huh?" Johnny D. said on the screen, pushing his too-long brown hair out of his eyes. "I guess you'll have figured it out by now. But I got you."

I got you. A chill ran through Jenna. Bile rose in the back of her throat. She convulsed, just a bit, and she was sure she was going to vomit. Quickly, she brought a hand up to cover her mouth, but nothing came out.

"Johnny, why?" she managed weakly.

But she didn't bother saying more than that. *What good would it do? He's done it to me already.* Jenna had learned that when people were as twisted as Johnny obviously was, there was no way to second-guess them, no reason even to wonder why they did the things they did.

Something else occurred to her then.

"You can't hear me, can you?" she said to the screen.

On the television, he went on, face in shadow in the darkened room. "I didn't even have to break in," he crowed. "Did it all from outside the house. Imagine that! Think about the ways in which that can be put to use. I can do it to entire neighborhoods, entire cities. I can set you off like a time bomb through your cable box. Hell, I've just done it. Now it's just wait and see to find out if it works on you.

"Do you think it will?"

Jenna started to breathe fast, panic overwhelming her. Tears began to well at the corners of her eyes, but she fought them back. The room seemed to crackle with electricity, as if the air itself were filled with menace. She put her hands to her mouth, whispered prayers, and tried to examine her head to see if there were any thoughts there that shouldn't be.

On the screen, there was a loud knocking. Johnny turned around fast, looking worried. Even afraid. With a startling suddenness, her cable came back on. An ad for Volkswagen.

Her eyes went to the clock on the VCR. 7:33. Her mother wouldn't be home for a couple of hours, at least. So if something happened to her, if she . . . lost control, at least her mom wouldn't be around. Jenna's chest hurt, as though the blood was pumping too fast through her heart. She got up and went to the phone.

Call Slick, she thought. *No, call Danny. No, too far away. Call . . .*

"Grillo," she said aloud.

He and Brody were outside, in the car.

Right outside.

Brody was bored. His hands lay across his belly, his head resting against the seat. Next to him, Grillo peered out the window at the Blake house. Nothing going on there. Brody didn't think there would be. By now, he figured, the DeAngelis kid would know that they were on to him. The way Brody had it worked out, the kid would either be on the run—and that couldn't last long, because all the reports indicated he had no real friends to speak of—or he'd be trying to contact somebody at the NSA or whatever, hoping for help.

223

From what Special Agent Dufresne had told them, the DeAngelis kid wasn't just a genius, he had a hell of an imagination, too. He thought he was going to be working for the Pentagon, or something.

Crazy thing was, if he weren't so detached from reality, the kid might actually have gotten somewhere with his ideas. At least, that was the way Brody figured it.

"Mike," Grillo said. "Do you think if I close my eyes and wish real hard, the coffee genie would come?"

Brody chuckled. "That trick never works. Why don't you go on up to the house and ask Jenna to make some? She's a good kid. I don't think she'd mind."

Grillo glanced at him, frowning. "I don't know. That seems a bit less than professional, don't you think?"

"Depends how bad you want coffee."

They received a call on their police radio, then. Grillo picked it up.

"You can go home now, detectives," the dispatcher said. "The FBI has your suspect in custody."

"Where'd they find him?" Grillo asked.

Brody had already started up the car. They were both looking forward to getting home at a decent hour.

"He'd rented out a basement from a neighbor," the dispatcher replied. "Special Agent Dufresne is expecting your call."

Grillo thanked the dispatcher, then glanced out the window, up at the house. He looked at Brody. "We should tell her it's over."

"Go on," Brody said. "I won't drive off without you. Not if you hurry, anyway."

With a chuckle, Grillo climbed out of the car. He pulled his jacket close around him and started across the lawn, shoes leaving prints in the newly fallen snow. Already the footprints left when he and Jenna had stood there talking, not long ago at all, had been eradicated completely. No sign at all.

Grillo marched up to the front steps and kicked the snow off his shoes before ringing the bell. He waited fifteen seconds before opening the storm door and knocking. When there was still no answer, he debated just going to the car and calling when they got back to the station. Jenna might be in the bathroom or the shower, or, for all he knew, she might have actually gone to bed already. It wasn't even eight o'clock, but that was possible.

He didn't want her to look outside and worry that there wasn't an officer there. Besides, if she'd fallen asleep, she couldn't have been sleeping very long.

Grillo pounded on the door again.

Then, from inside, he heard a muffled voice. "No . . . Go away. Just go away."

It was Jenna. *Accomplice* was the first word in Grillo's head. DeAngelis must have had someone else working with him.

"Brody!" he shouted.

He drew his gun, and then kicked at the door. At the third kick, the wooden frame shattered and the door swung open. Grillo didn't wait to see if Brody had heard him, or even if he was coming. He figured his partner would be backing him up any second.

Holding his breath, Grillo went in.

Slowly, he peered to the left, into the living room. Jenna was sitting in the room, the television on in front of her, holding a mug of something in her hands.

Grillo frowned. For a moment he wondered if he'd imagined the voice—the whole thing. But, then, Jenna wouldn't have just sat there while he broke the door down. Grillo glanced around him, wondering if someone else might be inside, if there was some trick to all of this.

"Jenna?" he ventured, and a stray thought crossed his mind.

She could be dead.

But, no. Even from here, he could see that she was moving, ever so slightly. Shivering, even.

"Get out," Jenna whispered.

"What's wrong?" he asked. "Look, Jenna, everything's okay now. They've got DeAngelis in custody. It's all over."

A tiny sound issued from Jenna's throat. A little like a laugh. A lot like choking.

Grillo moved around in front of her.

Jenna stared up at Detective Grillo, frozen inside herself. She couldn't even talk anymore. She'd tried. All she could do was feel. Feel the fury, and the hate, and the violence burning inside her.

"Hey, what is it?" Grillo asked gently. He bent down toward her.

With a grunt, she splashed the contents of her mug into his face. It wasn't that hot anymore, but Grillo swore and backed up. Jenna stood up fast, moved toward him, and brought the mug whipping around toward him. It shattered across his forehead, and the bridge of his nose, and Grillo staggered backward. He tried to bring his gun up, screaming something at her that she could barely hear over the sound of blood pumping through her. Jenna lunged at him, drove Grillo back against the television, her fingers grabbing the wrist of his right hand. She slammed it against the wood of the entertainment center until he dropped the gun.

Inside, she was screaming. Inside, she was crying in fear and horror and despair. But no tears came out. Only a sound like an inhuman growl.

Jenna kicked the gun away, then slashed at Grillo with the broken mug handle. He held up a hand to protect his face and she cut him.

He roared at her.

Next to the fireplace were black iron tools. Jenna reached for the poker, lifted it over her head, and began to beat Grillo with all of her strength. More than her strength.

She felt a grin stretch across her face, and that made it so much worse.

Crack! The poker struck Grillo's arm. Crack! Across his back. Crack! On the back of his head, and he went down hard on the carpet. Jenna stood over him, raised the poker again.

No! her mind screamed. She tried so hard, then, to stop. Her muscles felt as though they were tearing somehow. But she had no real control. None at all.

To her horror, she found that she did not want to

fight. Whatever tiny bit of her brain had been resisting the urge, the violence, the bloodlust, it was losing. It was as though she was blacking out, losing consciousness, but she knew that she wasn't. Jenna felt like she was fainting, but she wasn't going to fall.

With a laugh, she lost. What was left of Jenna felt a surge of triumph at the thought that she was about to kill this man, to crack his skull and see his brains spill onto the carpet.

Jenna was gone.

There was the crack of gunfire, but she didn't flinch. Didn't really even hear it. The poker came down.

Brody was there. He piled into Jenna from behind, driving her to the ground with his ample weight. She tried to strike out at him with the poker, but he tore it from her grasp and flung it across the room. Something shattered.

She raged. She spat. She tried to bite him.

But this time, it really *was* over. It took seven minutes for backup to arrive.

Two hours for the wildness to leave Jenna's eyes.

When it did, she couldn't remember anything after Grillo had knocked on the door.

But some part of her must have known.

How else to explain the sick feeling in the pit of her stomach, and the tears she couldn't seem to stop.

epilogue

Jenna felt like she was in the zoo, on the wrong side of the bars. She'd been in the hospital under observation for a day and a half, and there'd been an almost constant stream of visitors. A dozen different nurses and three different doctors had poked and prodded and given her a CAT scan and an MRI. For the first twenty-four hours, there was a uniformed police officer seated on a stool just outside her door. It made her feel weird, like she was in a movie or something.

Grillo and Brody had been in to talk to her, twice, and Jenna had been embarrassed both times. She felt horrible for what she'd done, and the few bruises she had were nothing compared to the facial lacerations, cracked ribs, and broken arm that Grillo had suffered. The first time she'd seen him, Jenna had wanted to throw up. The idea that she had been responsible for those injuries was almost more than she could grasp.

But Grillo had reminded her, several times, that she wasn't really responsible.

Thank God.

There would be no charges filed against her for the assault. Things seemed to be going in favor of the three murderers as well. No one was going to say that they didn't commit those crimes, but there was a great deal of evidence to say that they weren't responsible. Their lives had been destroyed, no question of that. Those they loved the most had been brutally murdered, and though they could not remember, they had to live with the knowledge that the blood was on their hands.

Their lawyers would argue that they had suffered enough, that they were just as much victims as those they had killed. The attorneys would plead not guilty by reason of temporary insanity, a strategy that, quite literally, *never* worked in Massachusetts. But everyone seemed to think that this time, things would work out differently.

After all, there was proof.

Grillo and Brody were funny, actually. They didn't come right out and thank Jenna for helping, and they made it clear that Lieutenant Donatello was still not completely happy, no matter what face he put on it, to have worked with a civilian, but they were also very kind to her. In the end, they had appreciated her input, and they seemed to like her. For her, that was enough.

Her mother was there almost constantly, of course. Several times doctors came in to Jenna's room, hoping to drag April away to perform one surgery or another. Only once did she agree to go, and then only because the patient was a thirteen-year-old girl who had become so attached to Dr. Blake in the weeks leading up to her planned surgery that she would have been terrified to learn that any other doctor was going to perform her operation.

Moira and Priya and Noah came in, of course. There was a long round of gossip, and then they told Jenna that she was the subject of plenty of gossip herself. The local papers had done a big story on her, and local television had covered it as well, though the media hadn't seemed to be really clear on exactly how the mind control had been accomplished.

Jenna couldn't explain it to them. Special Agent Dufresne had specifically asked her not to. John DeAngelis was in FBI custody, but all of his work had been confiscated. Any information related to it had been classified by the federal government.

She didn't like the sound of that, but there wasn't much she could do about it. Jenna promised herself she would follow up on what happened to Johnny D. after a while. He belonged in prison, no doubt about that. But she wondered if he would ever get there, or if he would be punished by being given the reward he'd always wanted. She knew she was probably being paranoid, but she couldn't help it. *Too much television*.

Priya had solidified her plans. She was going to work through the spring and summer, and she had been accepted to Northeastern for the fall. The idea of starting freshman year all over again seemed somehow comforting to her. It was a clean slate, and Jenna was happy for her.

An endless parade. All of them anxious for her, caring for her.

Wary of her.

That was the weird part. The fishbowl part. The behind-the-bars-in-the-zoo part. Every doctor or nurse or cop or friend who came in to see her kept a respectful distance, watching her carefully in case she should suddenly go rabid again, like some frothing animal or Viking berserker warrior. At first she found it troublesome, but in time it became merely amusing.

Only her mom didn't hesitate to be near her, to love and hold and kiss her. Jenna loved her all the more for that.

It was lunchtime on Saturday before they let her out. All of their tests had come to nothing. There wasn't a single oddity in her brain chemistry, and she had exhibited no violent tendencies during her hospital visit.

On Sunday, she spoke to Priya and Moira on the phone one last time before loading her bags into her father's car once again and heading back to Somerset. Hunter and Yoshiko weren't due back for a few more days, and the prospect of seeing them made her very happy—as did the knowledge that Dyson would be back in the office the next day, and she could tell him the whole story. Jenna was also looking forward to being back on track with work. Amid all the chaos, she had realized that, at least to her (though she thought maybe to him as well), she and Slick were pretty much Batman and Robin for dead folks.

That thought, which occurred to her as she drove the five-mile stretch of Route 2 on the way to Somerset, made her laugh out loud in the car. But the grin on her face as she drove the last few miles back to school—as she drove home—accompanied by ancient Rolling Stones on the radio, had nothing to do with any of that.

When she arrived at Sparrow Hall, Damon would be waiting for her.

Jenna was convinced that, back at school, and back in his arms, she could put the horror and tragedy of these sad holidays behind her.

In the early hours of Monday morning Jenna had a horrible nightmare about a vicious monster, and woke up in a silent scream, sweating, though the dorm was chilly that night.

In the dream, Jenna had been the monster.

It was a dream she would have, off and on, for months.

Turn the page for
a preview of
the next
Body of Evidence thriller

SKIN DEEP

Available October 2000

Brittany felt lucky.

It was the dead of winter in New England, the end of
January, the time of year when a long, romantic stroll is
usually out of the question. After Christmas break she
had returned to the Somerset University campus from
her home in West Virginia to find a barren, frigid waste-
land. According to some of her friends who lived in the
area, there had been snow in Boston for Christmas, and
then off and on for a week or so. It warmed up enough
the Wednesday after New Year's to melt what was there.
From that day on, there had been nothing but cold.

When classes resumed almost two weeks before,
Brittany and her friends spent most of their time
indoors, studying or watching movies. There were no
snowball fights, no sledding, no snowmen. It seemed too
cold even for snow. The campus lawns were frozen and
brittle, and it was harder than ever to make it to those
early-morning classes when all Brittany wanted to do
was pull her covers up higher and snuggle down deep.

On the other hand, if it hadn't been for the cold, she
might never have gotten to know Anthony better. Of
course she'd noticed him in the corridors of Bentley
Hall, and how could she not? He was a handsome guy

with a serious set to his features, broad-shouldered, and at least six foot three. Hard to miss, Anthony—or Ant, as his friends called him.

Brittany preferred "Anthony." She had no idea where "Ant" had come from, but she suspected it was a football thing. Anthony Williams played for the Somerset Colts. Though he was a freshman, she'd been told he had done very well that first year. Not that Brittany paid any attention to sports, but she had friends who did.

So she'd noticed him, sure. But she was a junior, two years older than Anthony. He spent a lot of his time either out of the dorm or hanging around with his crew. When she did see him on his own, studying in the common area or walking to class, he always seemed grim and silent. So quiet.

But in the first week of second semester that changed. Anthony was still far from talkative, but he *did* talk to her. Brittany was curled up in an uncomfortable lime-green chair in the common area reading *R.L.'s Dream* by Walter Mosley when Anthony came back from a class. She looked up and smiled, and he nodded and continued toward his room.

He came back.

In a shy, tentative way, he struck up a conversation about Mosley, and she discovered there was more to Anthony Williams than football and broad shoulders. Though he was a freshman, she felt in some ways that he was much older.

Since then a week had passed, a span of days in which nearly every moment she was not in class had been spent with Anthony. Nights out in Cambridge or in Lafford Square and a party at the arts house put them in public together, and some of her friends were a bit surprised that Brittany would date a freshman. But they didn't know him. Anthony didn't say much, but he had romance in his soul. They sat in Brittany's dorm room—a single, the benefit of being an upperclassman—and listened to music and talked only a little.

It was nice.

Over the weekend the temperatures had dipped so low that the campus was like a ghost town. Though January was supposed to mean a new beginning, Brittany found that in New England it was a depressing time of year. The winter blues came down hard on her. Or they usually did. The stretch between New Year's and Valentine's Day normally seemed eternal, and this cold would only have made it that much worse. But Anthony changed that.

Calm down, she told herself a dozen times. *It's only a little more than a week. They're all dogs inside. Not all the same kind of dog, but all dogs. Give him time to show it before you get silly over him.*

On Monday the weather changed abruptly. From eighteen degrees the day before—and much colder with the wind chill—it surged to nearly fifty by eleven in the morning. Overnight it only dropped to thirty. Then, this morning, Brittany woke up to snow.

Thirty-two degrees, according to the blonde on the morning news, just cold enough for snow. It came down all day, fat and lazy, and by dinnertime seven inches of white blanketed the campus. They ate fried scrod at Nadel Dining Hall, and then Anthony suggested they walk. She gazed up into his eyes and saw something simple and wonderful there. And he smiled sweetly, knowingly.

Now, hand in hand, they weaved through campus on freshly shoveled paths. Brittany shivered, and

Anthony put an arm around her and pulled her tightly to him. She had been all but buried in her winter coat, but tonight she wore only a black leather one her parents had given her for Christmas, as well as gloves and a scarf. Anthony had his Somerset Colts football jacket on, the nickname "Ant" sewn onto the breast.

Together, they were warm. The snow had all but ended, save for a few fat flakes that still twirled slowly to the ground. There was very little wind. The sky had begun to clear, and stars were peeking through. The evergreens and bare oaks that dotted the campus lawns were heavy with the fresh snow, which glistened in the light thrown by street lamps.

Wandering along the paved paths, they passed several other couples who apparently had the same idea and two groups of guys whose cabin fever had resulted in their getting very drunk the first day out of the cold snap. As they walked up the stairs cut into the hill that stretched between the President's House to the left and Mayer Library to the right, they heard wild laughter, cursing, and even a little shriek of pleasure.

"What are they doing over there?" Anthony asked.

"Traying."

"Traying?"

"They steal trays from one of the dining halls and sled on them."

Anthony frowned and tilted his head doubtfully to one side. Then he shook it slowly, as if to say, *Damn fools, that's not sledding*—which was almost exactly what Brittany had said the first time she saw students traying on the hill.

Under her breath, barely loud enough for Anthony to hear, she sang a verse of "Winter Wonderland," snatched from the ether to appear on her lips almost before her brain was aware of it. It was long past Christmas, but everything around them evoked the feeling of the holiday—or at least that archetypal holiday everyone wished it could be. The mythical Christmas, the winter wonderland.

She was astonished when Anthony began to sing the next verse. Though low, his voice was smooth and clear as crystal, a gospel voice, though she doubted he spent much time in church.

"What?" he asked when he caught her staring.

But Brittany could see a mischievous twinkle in his eye she had never noticed there before. Beneath the silence and the brooding and the thoughtful remarks, this was Anthony.

"You sing beautifully. Have you ever done anything with it? Choir or theater, anything?"

He shook his head. "That's all Brick's thing."

"Brick" was his roommate, James Bricker. Another one of those nicknames, like "Ant." Brittany understood what Anthony meant. Brick was into theater. Not necessarily musical theater, either. First semester, he'd been in a Somerset production of *A Soldier's Story*, and by all reports, he'd been excellent.

"Just because Brick does theater, that doesn't mean you can't do some singing yourself. You guys would probably have fun if you did it together sometime."

"More likely I'd kill him, spending that much time together."

Brittany laughed, but she could see it was not just a joke. The roommates spent a lot of time in each other's company as it was; Anthony loved Brick, but maybe they spent *enough* time together. She thought it was a shame.

Anthony had a nice singing voice, but it was obvious he had no real interest in doing anything with it.

"Well, maybe you can just sing to me," she suggested.

Without cracking a smile, or even glancing at her, his low voice, almost a whisper, went into Louis Armstrong's "What a Wonderful World." Brittany laughed and clung more tightly to him as they passed the library. It was built into the side of a slope, so that downhill, students could enter on the ground floor, but uphill, you could walk up three concrete steps and be on the roof.

At the top of the stairs, with the darkened façade of Brunswick Chapel looming over them, Brittany and Anthony paused. He stopped singing when their lips met. She felt a chill run through her that had nothing to do with winter, and then it turned to heat. When their lips parted, she lay her head on his chest.

"Let's go on the roof," she said.

He laughed and his chest rumbled against her cheek. "They haven't shoveled up there yet."

Brittany saw that he was right. Half a foot of snow draped the library roof in a shapeless white cover. Laughing, she held his hand tightly and pulled him toward it. With an indulgent shake of his head, he allowed her to lead him into the snow and up the steps to the roof.

The view was incredible. The snow had stopped completely now, and from the roof they could see the Boston skyline.

"It's beautiful," Brittany whispered.

Rather than respond with words, Anthony approached her from behind, encircling her with his arms. He kissed the top of her head, then bent to let his lips touch gently upon the goose-pimpled flesh of her neck.

She turned, rose up on the tips of her toes, and kissed him more deeply. Minutes passed. She took her gloves off so she could feel the heat of his hands, touch his face, reach inside his jacket for his warmth. His fingers twined in her hair, caressed her face, and as she studied his eyes, she saw—felt—him opening up to her. Beneath that quiet air, she knew there was something very special. She'd been allowed glimpses of it, but Brittany was starting to think she wanted it all. It worried her. She wasn't used to needing anybody, and she didn't think they'd been together long enough for her to need Anthony.

"You're something," she whispered to him.

He only smiled, and kissed her again.

"Maybe we should pick this up back at the dorm?" she suggested.

"Wherever you go, I'll follow," he told her.

God, does that sound like a line. But somehow she knew it wasn't. She gazed up into his eyes for several heartbeats, then sighed, smiled softly, and kissed him again.

"Animals."

With the snow so thick, neither of them had heard anyone approaching. When he spoke, they both turned instantly, alarmed not merely by his presence but by the tone of his voice. So angry. So hostile. So filled with . . . what?

Disgust.

Anthony didn't have a chance to speak. Even as they turned, the shovel cut across the space between them. It was an old-fashioned wood-and-iron tool with a square blade, more appropriate for digging earth than snow. The flat of the blade slammed into Anthony's face with a sickening crack, splaying his shattered nose and spattering blood into the air.

Crimson-spattered snow.

Anthony went down, groaning.

It was a white guy, a student, if his Somerset jacket was any indication. Dark hair, but other than that there was nothing remarkable about him. Except for the shovel in his hands.

Brittany screamed for Anthony to get up, screamed at the son of a bitch who had just attacked him. Screamed for help.

She heard someone respond, not far off. People calling out. Help on the way.

"Your kind just can't keep your hands off each other, can you?" the guy with the shovel said. "Animals, I swear."

Anthony roared, started to lunge at him from the snow. The shovel came down again, striking his skull with a dull thud. Brittany screamed for help, and once again, someone called a reply. They were coming. They were close.

He went at Anthony again, but she wouldn't let him. Brittany grabbed him from behind, her hands tight on his throat, trying to choke him. Her fingernails dug into his flesh, drawing blood, and he cried out in anger and pain. An elbow rammed into her stomach and she almost threw up, tumbling into the snow.

She stood quickly. He had forgotten about Anthony and was focused only on her now. "Don't come near me," she snarled, backing away, hands in front of her.

He broke her hands with the shovel. As she cried out in pain, he drove it blade-first into her gut. Her leather jacket saved her from being cut open, but the wind was forced from her lungs.

Help's on the way, she told herself again. She heard them, so close.

Not close enough.

The shovel fell silently into the powdery snow as he rushed at her. He drove her backward and slammed her spine against the waist-high concrete retaining wall that ran around the edges of the roof. One more shove, and she was over.

For a single eyeblink, she held on with the tips of the fingers of her left hand. Below, the newly shoveled courtyard in front of the library's entrance had just a dusting of snow covering it.

Brittany didn't scream. The drop from the library's roof to the courtyard was more than thirty feet. Even as she fell, the powdered concrete rushing up to shatter her bones, she could hear the shouts of people who were coming to try to save her. Her sorrow welled up in her, the knowledge that they had been so close bringing a tear to her eye.

It never fell.

Look for the next
Body of Evidence **thriller**
SKIN DEEP
by Christopher Golden
Available from Pocket Pulse
October 2000

about the author

CHRISTOPHER GOLDEN is the award-winning, *L.A.
Times*–bestselling author of such novels as *Strange-
wood* and the three-volume *Shadow Saga*; *Hellboy: The
Lost Army*; and the *Body of Evidence* series of teen
thrillers (including *Thief of Hearts* and *Soul Survivor*),
which is currently being developed for television by
Viacom.

He has also written or cowritten a great many
books, both novels and nonfiction, based on the popular TV series *Buffy the Vampire Slayer* and the world's
number one comic book, *X-Men*.

Golden's comic-book work includes the recent
Wolverine/Punisher: Revelation, and stints on the *The
Crow* and *Spider-Man Unlimited*. Upcoming projects
include a run on *Buffy the Vampire Slayer*; *Batman: Real
Worlds* for DC; and the ongoing monthly *Angel* series,
tying into the Buffy television spinoff.

The editor of the Bram Stoker Award–winning
book of criticism *CUT!: Horror Writers on Horror Film*,
he has written articles for *The Boston Herald*, *Disney
Adventures*, and *Billboard*, among others, and was a regular columnist for the worldwide service BPI Entertainment News Wire.

Before becoming a full-time writer, he was licensing manager for *Billboard* magazine in New York, where he worked on Fox Television's *Billboard Music Awards* and *American Top 40* radio, among many other projects.

Golden was born and raised in Massachusetts, where he still lives with his family. He graduated from Tufts University. He is currently at work on his next novel, *Straight on 'til Morning*. Please visit him at *www.christophergolden.com*.